STEEL

ALSO BY KATHLEEN NOVAK

Do Not Find Me

The Autobiography of Corrine Bernard: A Novel

Rare Birds

STEEL

KATHLEEN NOVAK

Library of Congress Control Number: 2021908220

FIC 019000 Fiction/Literary
FIC 014000 Fiction/Historic
FIC 027050 Fiction/Romance

Novak, Kathleen, author.

STEEL / Kathleen Novak

ISBN: 978-1-7342298-9-9

Cover design: Lon Kirschner @ Kirschner Design

BLACK CAT 🐱 TEXT

MINNEAPOLIS, MINNESOTA

for my father

STEEL

The gun hung by the door where the men could see it.

The men were boarders who worked in the mine dug wide as a crater not even a mile from that door. They had old country names like Milanović and Scippioni and nicknames like Yum-Yum and Stick. They came from everywhere for work and they worked in the mines to make money. The work was dark and dangerous. The men moved twenty-five million tons of ore with steam shovels and steam locomotives, all the smoke of steam and the heaps of discarded ore that rose like barren mountains around them.

The gun hung on the entry wall as a warning. The couple who ran the boarding house had daughters, good looking enough and sweet, those daughters, and their father, Joseph Babić, known as Jocco, was a foreman in the mines, a supervisor of men. He knew men. His wife, Marie, kept chickens, a cow, always a pig. She baked thirteen loaves of bread every day, fed the men, cared for them. She did not like the gun by the door, but it wasn't hers to say. She boiled pots of water for tea, kept an eye out. The miners were boys to her, and some spoke her language from home, so she kept an eye out.

Marie Babić had given birth to a baby almost every other year for twenty years. The first died in months. The couple lived in Fort Francis then and a crow came to their window. That's how she'd known the baby would die. She'd known without understanding, so much the way in the new world, knowing and not quite understanding. Three more children died before one made it past two years to four years to eight to twelve, and the girls that came after and the little boys after that, all marching into real life past sickness and cold, bearing their names high like flags. Margaret, Anna, Catherine, Peter and John, Nicolas, George, and Helen. But the first was Anthony, Tony, named for the saint of what is lost. He was her first who lived. He went to school, played ball, did well. Tony always did so well.

Jocco spoke English, wrote longhand with the flow and loops of intelligence, and passed his citizenship tests with ease. In the mine, he ran the men who laid tracks so locomotives could move out the ore. Before the miners dug, Jocco's men laid the tracks. They were the dregs. You didn't need to be anything to heft steel tracks and pound rivets into the rails all day. It was Jocco's job to keep them working. When the long shift was done, he went home to all his children, a worn-out wife, and ten boarders. Often he went home drunk. But he always went home.

The boarders washed up before supper in respect to Marie Babić. She took care of them, shooed them with her hands, covered her mouth when she laughed, smelled always of soap as their own mothers had. Marie and her daughters pulled their wavy dark hair back and twisted and pinned it. That's how women were meant to look. The girls had sturdy, corseted waists. They loved to dance. That is why Jocco Babić kept a gun by the door, a war issue, six-shot pistol made of steel.

The gun was made of steel.

Nobody touched it.

KATHLEEN NOVAK

STEEL

ONE

i.

He wasn't a cop when he was a boarder. He was a Croatian miner named Luka, and he was Marie's favorite. He'd come from a village near hers. She thought she might have known his mother when they were young, but maybe not. Maybe she was imagining that because she liked Luka so much, always a nice face, always hello Mrs. Babić.

He'd come to them in 1922, just after Johnny was born, but before Nicholas. Her Tony had no big brothers, only baby brothers, so he hung around this Luka, all grown and sitting at their table.

"You see my muscles, Luka?"

"Where you going now, Luka?"

"Want to play catch?"

It went on for two years, Luka at meals, Luka in the muddy street, throwing balls, spinning tales.

He told the boy he wanted to be a cop and fight crime. He wanted to move to a city called Chicago. It was an idea he had, stories he'd heard. He saved his money in a leather pouch his grandfather had sewn for him, and which he hid every day from the other boarders, changing spots in and around his bunk, tucking it into his pants, anything to save money for this place Chicago, where he would be a cop and fight crime.

He left in 1924, promising to write. But it took almost another year before they heard from him and then the news was astonishing. "Luka's a cop!" Tony relayed to his mother, who could not read English. "He's a Chicago cop now and he says someday I can visit him. He says it right here, right here it says, I'd like Tony to come and stay with me sometime. In the summer when there's no school. I'd like to show him Chicago." That's what Luka wrote and those were the words that sunk so deeply into Tony's mind he thought them preordained, part of life's plan, his destiny.

Tony Babić was fourteen then. His mother was not going to let him travel to Chicago to see a cop, even if that cop was Luka who had been like a son and had come from a village near to her village. And Jocco was not about to spend his money on a train ticket for a boy with big ideas. The mines were expanding, the town still moving part and parcel, a new immigrant law keeping workers out. Jocco had no time for big ideas.

But Tony was an industrious boy. He kept the letter. He wrote back and began a paper friendship with his hero, Luka, the Chicago cop. Dear Luka, he'd write, feeling important in the world, writing to a cop, sealing the envelope, putting on the stamp, and sending it off to a city he could not even imagine.

Tony's world was the Morris Location, one of many mining settlements built along the edges of the vast Hull Rust Mine, settlements that kept men, most who had no transportation, close to the mine where they worked. The Morris Location was home to mining company supervisors like Jocco, for large mining families whose kids were Tony's friends, tough, scrappy, fun kids. The houses sat on a grid, most of them large, though not necessarily permanent looking, because the mining company had built them and, eventually, the mining company would tear them down. But in that decade of the 1920s, the Morris Location was Tony's neighborhood. It was what he knew. A mile away was the new high school like a castle in the middle of town. He knew that too.

But the world of Luka in Chicago was completely unknown. What does a cop do? Tony asked in his first letter. Tell me what you do. He wrote the words in his best penmanship, each letter crafted onto the paper, one word flowing to the next. Tell me what you do. Do you have a badge, a club, a gun? And always, in weeks or months, a letter would arrive in return. Most of the cops he knew in Chicago were Irish, Luka said. Who ever heard of a Croatian cop in Chicago? Yes, he wore a badge shaped like a star with the words Police and Chicago engraved into the metal. He carried a gun. It took some getting used to, he wrote to Tony, that heavy gun around his hip, but it was a risky time for cops in Chicago. Gangsters shot without worry of recrimination. They were lawless and unbounded. But, Tony noted, Luka never said he was afraid.

"Luka goes to a city of shooters?" Marie asked her son. She could not think of it, this shooting.

"He wears a badge, Ma," Tony chanted. What would it feel like to wear a badge shaped like a star?

Say hi to your mother, Luka said at the end of every letter. Tell her I'm fine. I'll see her again sometime. Tell her. And Tony would tell her. He'd go on and on about Luka to his mother as she moved around her kitchen cooking, always cooking something.

In 1927, Luka wrote a serious letter to Marie and Jocco. He said that Tony should see more of the world than the iron mining towns of Northern Minnesota. He said he would send a train ticket for Tony to come in June and spend three days with him. Luka would take time off to be with the boy, he would not leave him alone, Tony would be safe, and he'd learn, and he'd never forget the trip all his life. That's what Luka said because that's what he believed. Young men needed to know the world. What was it to be born in a small, northern town and go nowhere, see nothing, work in a mine for the rest of his life? Luka was not even thirty years old and he had traveled from Croatia to Boston Harbor, to Minnesota and Chicago. That's why he was a good cop. He knew people. He knew that wherever you went there was something familiar and something so different it took you time to understand. But after you understood, you fit into the picture and you could be a good miner or cop or whatever you wanted to be. You looked into people's eyes. You saw something the same and something different and you knew what it meant. Luka wanted that for Tony. Wanted to pass along what he'd learned to Tony.

Yet such an argument! Jocco was wild, Marie fretful. Tony's sisters had their reasons for him to not leave, his kid brothers tugged on his sleeves like he'd be gone for a century. Spring rains turned the entire Morris Location to mud and still no decision was made. Then Luka wrote again, this time on a postcard showing Michigan Avenue. Looking north to the lake, the caption said. This postcard gave the family a very different notion of Chicago. There it was in the colored photograph with such buildings, high and dignified, some more than twenty stories Tony counted, and the far blue of the lake at the end of the street. It didn't look risky or unruly, but stately. Rich and promising.

Jocco took it all in, the refinement and largeness, cars on the boulevard, paved streets and walkways. Go, he told his son. Go see Luka. He dug in his steamer trunk, kept at the foot of the bed he shared with Marie, and took out two silver dollars from the cigar box at the bottom of the trunk. He slipped these into Tony's hand without a word. He narrowed his eyes and gripped the boy's shoulder. That was it.

Tony had to walk to the train station with his one bag, a frayed, shabby thing some boarder had left behind, but with every step, his shoulders lifted higher and his stride became more sure. Behind him his mother sat on a chair in her kitchen, covered her eyes with her apron and wept. He was her oldest boy, the first one who lived. Her daughter Margaret told her Luka would take care of Tony, not to worry, Ma. But what was that? Luka was just a boy too.

It took Tony a whole day to get to Union Station in Chicago. From home, he'd traveled on a single passenger car hitched to a freight train rolling toward the port of Duluth. In Duluth, he'd boarded a second train to Minneapolis and changed once more for Chicago.

Then there he was. The depot's ceiling curving to an unbelievable height overhead, the stairs sweeping wide, a hundred stairs at least, businesses tucked into the building's shadows. Newspapers and magazines over there. Tobacco and candies here. A barbershop. The whole of the Morris Location could fit under the dome of Union Station, he was sure of it. Even his grand European-style high school did not have this scale, this enormity, did not make this statement of presence. Here you are, the place hollered. In Chicago, the likes of which you have not seen before.

Luka spotted the boy immediately, standing near the darkly stained wooden benches, mouth agape and eyes roving. He'd grown so much in three years, his jaw square now, his hands too large for his frame.

"Tony!" the cop called out. "Over here, Tony!"

He grasped the boy with both arms, felt the substance there, a young man now, a football player, his mother's eldest son.

"Luka, you're just the same," Tony blurted out in surprise, for sure enough Luka the cop in his summer suit coat didn't look any different than Luka the miner in his heavy denim overalls. Same close haircut. Same rosy skin, big smile, clear eyes. "Where's your badge?"

Luka laughed. "I'm not working today, Tony. I'll show you my gear later." He ushered the boy out into the steamy Chicago night. After walking a few blocks, they got onto a bus that took them down that same street Tony had seen on Luka's color postcard. But now lights were on in those tall buildings, and the night sky hovered hazy above. "You can't see half the stars here, Luka."

"City lights, Tony. They blur out heaven." Luka smiled an old-seeming smile that wasn't like anything Tony had seen on him before. When they got off the bus, Luka took Tony's bag and carried it to a corner café near Lincoln Park. He held open the door, saying, "You are now entering one of the best cop hangouts on the North Side, Tony." They stepped into a noisy, smoky, smelly, and high-spirited room full of men who almost looked like Luka, young, lively, and handsome in a rough way, with those open smiles like Luka always had for Mrs. Babić.

"They're cops?" Tony whispered. "Really?" The two sat at a worn wooden table, pulled out beat-up chairs that scraped against the floor. "Do all these guys really shoot people?"

It didn't seem possible. They could have been a football team, an older league of some kind. Tony had never imagined a room of cops would be tossing back sodas and telling jokes. Or whatever they were telling. They thought it was funny whatever they were telling.

"Thing is," Luka said, "cops just like being with cops. We're a different breed. Not like other people, Tony, and when we're not working, we just want to be with each other. We don't want regular folks asking us questions or telling us problems. We just want to let loose. We live in danger and we never know."

"Never know what?"

"Exactly, Tony. We never know what."

Over the next two days, Luka took Tony Babić for a walk down Michigan Avenue and for rides on the elevated trains that criss-crossed the city. They sat on the sand staring out across the wild of Lake Michigan and hung over a bridge to watch the Chicago River flow beneath them. Tony gawked at every building he saw, turrets and gargoyles, massive structures towering. They went to the zoo. "Nobody will believe this," Tony said, standing in front of the tiger, heavy and bored, with eyes saying to leave him alone. Wild animals he knew stayed wild.

In Luka's one-room sweltering apartment, Tony got to see the cop's badge and holster and gun. He handled them all under Luka's watch. Felt the heft of the gun, the cumbersome thick leather of the holster. He held the badge to his chest. "I should be a cop," the boy announced. "You love it, don't you, Luka? You'd never come back to be a miner, would you?"

"Don't think about all this yet, Tony. You're a smart kid. Stay in school. See what happens."

"But you're happy, aren't you, Luka?"

The young cop was thinking about the gangsters who roamed unrestrained on the streets of Chicago, running half the services in the city from their back rooms, bootlegging and gambling and shooting anyone who got in their way. "You hear about Al Capone, Tony?"

"Sure. You guys going to get him?"

"Sometimes we think he runs the town. There's lots of guys like him, Tony, hundreds of them. They're killers. And half the time they're killing each other. Just this year we had Sam Valante from one gang killed, Johnny Costanaro from another, then Lefty Koncil, a month ago Vince Drucci from the North Side—one of our cops got him, then there was Jimmy D'Amato." Luka ticked them off, name after name, sticking up a single finger for each gangster. "See what I'm telling you? You never know what."

Tony squirmed around on his chair, every inch of him moving. "You're fighting crime, Luka. Like you always said. Like you always said you would."

"You want some ice cream, Tony? Let's go out and get some ice cream."

Riding back to Minnesota the next day Tony had many hours to think about what he'd seen and done and heard. Every time he looked out the dirty train window, it seemed the world was becoming smaller and then smaller again. The depot in his hometown wasn't even as big as that cop café by Lincoln Park.

He trudged along the Hull Rust Mine to the Morris Location, more worldly and awed than he had ever thought he'd be. He'd been near the face of crime and heard the rough laugh of the just in the city of Chicago.

ii.

Vita. She had the kind of hair that could not be contained. The wisps took off in different directions around her face. Every time Tony saw that girl, his insides lurched. Hi Vita was all he could say, passing at school, stopping by her family's grocery. Hi Vita. Big deal.

But maybe that was before. Maybe that was the Tony Babić who had not traveled all the way to Chicago by himself and sat in a room full of cops. Cops who wore badges and guns and went after the biggest gangsters of all time, like Al Capone.

"Let me tell you about Al Capone," Luka had said. "He'd shoot an old woman if she crossed him. Even an Italian old woman." That's what Luka had said. And now Tony was a guy who knew those things. Had touched the badge, held the gun.

A bell on the door jangled when Tony walked into Marković's Grocery. There was that smell. Pork sausage and sweets, tobacco and bleach. "Hi Vita" he said as he always did, as if he weren't new now. "You having a good summer?"

Oh god, she was pretty. Not too tall, not too skinny, just everything right.

"It's fine, Tony. I work a lot. You need something?"

The store felt so hot, flies hanging onto the screen door, all those smells. Only a minute went by, seconds really, while he thought about what to say, lost in Vita there wearing a pale brown dress with a small collar and an apron over the dress in blue, that blue of overalls. Not dark or light, but perfect for her, for her eyes and hair.

"My ma could use something," Tony said at last. He nodded as if he knew what his ma could use, his mind flipping about, trying to settle like the dizzy flies outside the door.

"My ma likes yours, did you know that? They're friends. Old country ties I guess."

Tony kept nodding, good fortune coming his way that the mothers are friends. "I didn't know," he said.

"Oh yeah. It's the truth." Then Vita smiled like the truth. Not a flashy smile or a stingy smile. An easy, round sort of smile.

"I didn't know," he said again. He couldn't take his eyes off Vita behind the counter.

"Your mother need bananas, Tony? We got nice ones today."

He saw those bananas in a wooden crate on the floor. His mother didn't buy bananas until they were half brown and cheap. Then she'd make banana bread and cut fat slices hot with butter. That would be lunch. The Babićs and their boarders didn't eat bright yellow bananas like the ones on the floor by Vita.

"Maybe she could use sugar," he said.

"Oh sure. Sugar."

Vita walked across the store to a shelf where she hoisted down a sack of sugar. She had a hole in her stocking—large enough for Tony to see her skin, pale under the thick cotton sock. The heels on her shoes were worn down the way his were, scuffed at the toe and worn at the heel, the soles probably thin as communion wafers.

"You having a good summer?" he found himself asking again.

Vita came his way carrying the heavy sack of sugar, walked past him and around to her side of the grocery store counter, ignoring his question. "It's a dollar. You want to pay now—or does your ma have credit?"

Tony had no idea. Jocco Babić disapproved of credit, believed in cash, rolls and tin boxes of cash. Loose change counted to the penny. "You hold that sugar, Vita. I'll be back." He smiled too hard at her, as if his teeth might pop out. He hadn't thought this through, this visit to the Marković store to see if Vita was there. "I'll be back. Don't go anywhere, all right?"

She really laughed at that one. "Where would I go, Tony?" she called, but he had already slammed through the screen door and was rounding the corner. She had never been to Morris Location, but she knew where it was, on the east side of the Hull Rust, maybe a mile away. She wrapped the sugar in brown paper, tied it with string, and wrote "Babić" on it. Then she set it beneath the counter. He was a nice boy, that Tony. It seemed like he was getting better looking over time.

Vita and her friends kept a quiet watch on the boys they knew. Croatian boys mostly and Italians. Serbians not so much. Roundheads almost never, who were all Protestants—Swedes, Finns, and Norwegians—and off limits. "They always think they're better than everyone else," Vita's older sister had instructed. And you could never marry a Protestant anyway.

Vita knew Jewish girls in school and they were fun. But she didn't know the Jewish boys. Only the Jewish girls knew the Jewish boys. But the Catholics and Jews got along. Old religions and good food, her mother would say.

Tony Babić had always been a boy who stayed out of trouble, Vita knew that. Now he was on the football team and smart. When he came back, she'd tell him about going to Bennet Park to listen to the City Band. The band wasn't much, some teachers and junior college students on their horns and fiddles, but they tried. And people gathered to hear them which was fun. Vita liked going to the park.

Sitting on the stool behind her family's grocery counter, Vita wandered into her own fantasy of meeting Tony Babić at the park, telling him what she knew about the music, which she did not really, but in a daydream you could know anything you wanted to know, be smarter than ever. Tony would reach for her hand.

He'd tell her a story from Morris Location where she'd heard they played in the street having great good times that those in town didn't have. He'd hold her hand and go on with his story while the City Band played "If You Knew Susie Like I Know Susie" or "Bye Bye Blackbird."

There would be so many stars they'd light up the night like Christmas and beyond them would be that dark blue, deep blue sky of the North. "Heh, Tony," she'd say pointing to Venus on her throne in the heavens, "I could be named after that star."

"Vita! Ma says come upstairs and help with the jelly." Her younger brother, Billy, stood in the back doorway. "I'll take over here."

Eyes clouded, she gave up her dream and the anticipation of Tony Babić's return and relinquished the store to her brother. "One of the boys from Morris Location is coming back to get that package of sugar under the counter," she said with a last fast glance at the door where Tony Babić would reenter only to find her gone.

iii.

Bennet Park had everything. Its fifty acres of land held pavilions and playgrounds, a golf course, a baseball field, bocce and horse-shoe courts, picnic tables, even imported exotic plants. Vita, along with everyone in her neighborhood, had watched the park emerge over four years following the town's relocation from immediately south of the mine to a mile farther south. She'd been a child then, awed by the dirt movers and construction just blocks from their family store. Workers would come by for her mother's pastries or bottles of soda. "Good for business," her father would say.

The town's move by the mining company had been very good for the Markovićs' business, pushing the town in their direction and expanding the population of the Brooklyn Addition where they lived and the nearby locations like Pool, Kitzville, the Webb, and Morris. Vita's father had arrived in town twenty years earlier, worked in the mine, and gradually turned the downstairs of their house into a grocery. He built his own shelves, sold his wife's pastries, then made connections to buy produce and packaged goods until, in 1920, he put a small advertisement in the parish bulletin:

Markovič's Grocery
Now Open Daily

It was a family business. Vita, her siblings, her mother, and father all spent some time every day working in the grocery. It was a two-story, brown stucco, corner store. And it was just blocks from the park.

Vita and her friends showed up at the park to be seen. They'd fuss with their hair and pinch their cheeks, pull themselves tall and pretend they did not notice or care that they were young and pretty, that maybe they were wearing just the right color dress or had splashed rosewater from the five and dime at their neck and wrists.

Most of the boys their age were less interested in girls in summer dresses than in winning a horseshoe match or pitching a no-hitter at the baseball field. The boys their age seemed to most want other boys to notice them, as if that kind of recognition was the key to popularity and success.

Still there were moments. Sideways glances and flushed faces. And these the girls absorbed, took into themselves like cold drinks in the hot sun. But on this night after Tony Babič's visit to the grocery, Vita searched only for his face in one group of boys after another. Eddie Maras and the Brooklyn boys, Jimmy Andrucci and his Park Addition friends, Angie Antonelli with the kids from Alice Addition, boys in ties and boys in suspenders, in caps and boaters, a few with hair slicked flat by Brilliantine wearing no hats at all.

Vita walked with her two best friends, Kitty and Marguerite, Kitty always alert to what was going on around them and Marguerite drifting along in odd thoughts all her own, contemplating the flowers or the clouds or the thicket of pine trees up ahead. "Where is everyone from the locations I wonder?" Vita asked, her voice carefully nonchalant, a trifle tossed on the evening breeze.

Marguerite seemed not to hear her. Kitty didn't answer until she had satisfied herself that none of the Alice boys were watching them walk by. "Probably too far to come."

"I wonder what they do then." Vita speculated, imagining robust skirmishes with boys and girls together, shoulders bumping—or more—nicknames and teases like she'd witnessed sometimes on the lawn outside of school. "Suppose they make their own fun."

She wanted to hear what Kitty thought, but Kitty was fixated on the Italian boys, and on the cadence of her walk, the exact angle of her profile, the swish of her skirt at her knees. Which left Vita to speculate on her own. It wasn't that she wanted a boyfriend, exactly. Her father would not approve of a boyfriend. But to have a boy who liked you the most, who maybe repeated his words the way Tony Babić had in the store that day, trying to say the right thing as if there even was a right thing to say. That would be something. That would make the long days shorter. She could write notes to slip to him in the hallway at school. Steal one of her mother's pastries for him now and then.

"What are you smiling about?" Kitty nudged at Vita's side. "Who do you see?" Her eyes darted all about looking for the recipient of Vita's smile.

"Nothing. Just thinking about something funny."

"What? What's funny?"

They were wandering one of the walkways that trailed through the park. Behind them the City Band was eking out the Charleston. "I love this song," Vita called out. "I wish I knew how to do the Charleston, don't you, Kitty?"

But just then Sammy Bretto from Brooklyn said hello as he passed them, and Kitty's face smoothed into a trance. "Did you see that?" she whispered to her friends. "Did you see that? Did you see that look he gave me?"

"He's my neighbor," Marguerite said out of the blue. "That's why he smiled."

Kitty did not reply. She'd seen Sammy's eyes squarely on her own, his brown eyes looking right at her. "Let's go watch horseshoes," she suggested, calculating that to get to the horseshoe courts they'd need to circle back and possibly encounter Sammy Bretto again.

Marguerite shrugged, but Vita didn't hear anything Kitty had just said. Her eyes were on a boy and girl she didn't know, sitting on the merry-go-round, heads tucked together and oblivious to the world.

iv.

Jocco Babić had spent almost twenty years working the Hull Rust Mahoning Mine. He'd seen it through the days when it was a string of smaller mines east to west, when the boundaries between those were eliminated to form the wide, open pit it was now. He'd spent his adult life in the dust of iron ore, the layered reds of minerals, the piles of rock and edges of steel rails.

Men came and went. Short-timers like Luka moved on to some other dream. Transient laborers showed up when the mines boomed, made their money, and left to follow opportunity wherever it took them next. In his time, Jocco had seen workers from half the world gravitate to the Mesabi Range of Northern Minnesota—from northern, southern, and eastern Europe, Greece, Russia, and China. Most of them spoke no English. Yet everyone learned what to do, how to dig or hoist, how to operate heavy trucks and trains. They kept to their own kind, did their work, took their pay.

The Morris Location was built at the northeastern edge of the mine. Jocco's family walked that edge to get to the rest of town, to Brooklyn, the downtown stores, to the high school, city hall, and church. Life circled the Hull Rust. And in turn, the mine expanded and thrived in their midst. Ore was mined and crushed and loaded onto trains, carried to Lake Superior, and sent out across the Great Lakes to steel mill towns everywhere. That was its magnitude. The largeness of what they did. The ore went everywhere.

Most of the immigrant workers became Americans. Even Jocco's wife, Marie, who had never had any education, who had not learned to read or write anything anywhere, was now staring at English words on the papers, listening to her children's coaxing, "Ma, you write it like this, do it this way, Ma," letting them guide her hand as she held the pen to practice forming Marie Babić, Marie Babić fifty times on the paper, her name in letters she was just discovering were hers.

The Hull Rust Mahoning was an open pit many miles across and even more miles long. The men didn't have to work underground because the ore was so close to the surface, waiting there to be found. Waiting to be extracted, as management would say. Often Jocco looked up from the layers of ore to see the northern sky, more vast than the mine, and pure—limitless and pure. There he was, between the great pit and heaven.

He had five sons. They were all Americans. They would learn to read and write, be smart like Tony who took on books two inches thick and remembered what he'd learned. A math he called algebra. A science he called biology. Ten-dollar words like reassignment, belligerent, and liquefy.

"Where you ever going to say those things?"

"Anywhere, Pa. Anywhere."

So that was it. Knowledge. Where would Tony and his brothers take their knowledge, those words and numbers and the dates of many wars? Over to the Hull Rust Mahoning? Down the layered levels of iron ore to a ten-ton truck or extractor? Was that their future? Ore dust and lunch pails?

Jocco wasn't sure. Education was good, was fine. But Jocco had a paycheck, a pension, a place, a house built by U.S. Steel, some stability. That's what came with the ore dust.

"You going to get me a job in the mine, Pa?"

Tony had asked this too many times to count. Only now the boy had this other idea, this cop idea, to follow Luka to the city and round up gangsters. "Luka's going to get Al Capone someday, Pa. Wait and see. Just wait and see."

Jocco would shake his head. No point in the argument. Wait and see was half of life on any day. It didn't take school to figure that one. Even Marie without a day of school behind her knew about wait and see. Like Jocco, she'd always known that much.

For Tony, the Hull Rust Mahoning existed in perpetuity. It was like the big lake in Luka's Chicago, not just part of the landscape, but part of what the place meant and why it was there at all. Without the Hull Rust Mahoning, what? Only tundra, pine ridges, thousands of lakes, and the Northern Lights. There would be no town with its assembled residents, grids of paved roads lined by homes and businesses, rows of streetlights, fire hydrants at the corner curbs. There would be no Morris, Webb, Brooklyn, or Kelly Lake.

There would be no Vita Marković.

All thoughts in Tony's mind that summer circled around the image of Vita in her blue apron reaching for a sack of sugar on the shelf, a hole in her stocking and the heels of her shoes worn away.

When he'd returned to the grocery that day, the same flies buzzed at the screen and the same dusty heat filled the store. But Vita's brother, Billy, stood behind the counter chatting to Tony about something he no longer remembered, football maybe, the start of the football season soon. The boy handed Tony a brown package with Babić written in pencil on the top.

"Where is everyone?" Tony ventured to ask.

"Oh yeah," Billy chuckled. "Too busy to mind the store, that's where they are."

"Tell them hi," Tony said, and the brother nodded agreeably, a nice boy taking care of business, old beyond his years, responsible, and oblivious to the pains of love.

There had been no more to say or wish for and Tony had gone home. After that, he stopped by on three more errands for his mother, all orchestrated, even cajoled by "anything you need over at Marković's store, Ma?" Marie Babić had pushed her eldest child out of her way countless times that summer, impatient with his need to buy things at Marković's Grocery. "Go now," she'd say. "Go feed the pig. Sweep the steps. Go you."

And when he did convince her of some dire need, he would half run along the edge of the Hull Rust on his way to see Vita behind the counter of her family's store. But he never found her there again. He purchased whatever his mother had asked, roamed the small store stalling for as long as was polite and left, listening to the bells jangle against the door as he went.

The Hull Rust Mahoning mine had not become any larger that summer. It remained the same on its eastern border as it had been for the last several years. Long enough for the brambles to grow along its edges and wild blueberries as well. But it seemed larger than ever to Tony. The Morris Location where he lived was on one end. Vita Marković was on the other.

v.

School put an end to summer. Tony hurried from one class to another, scanning the crowds for Vita's wayward curls and pretty face. He'd picture her in that light brown dress with the round collar. Sometimes he'd search for her blue apron, too, but he knew that was silly—though you never could guess what girls were going to do. Or think, or wear.

Tony's high school and its grounds, built by the mining company in compensation for moving the entire town, covered four city blocks and included a gymnasium, indoor swimming pool, a football field with stands, a music room, fully appointed home economics kitchens, a tool shop, a massive study hall, a library, and a theater with velvet seats, the largest vaudeville organ in the country, and chandeliers shipped from Czechoslovakia. This grandeur was not lost on the students. Every school day they climbed marble steps, grasped brass stair rails, and moved in expansive spaces surrounded by authentic art, hand-painted murals, and polished floors.

The students lived within it, absorbed it or did not as they made their way from place to place, hurried from the lower-level class-rooms up stately staircases to the fourth-level classrooms. To get from the east wing to the west wing of the school might take five minutes of concentrated effort dodging other students in the wide hallways. For Tony's last class of the day, he had to travel from downstairs to upstairs and from east to west. Charging head down on the second Friday of the school year, he turned too quickly rounding the corner of the stairs and knocked into someone whose books went flying onto the floor in front of him. He dove down to gather them, not even seeing the worn shoes and mended stockings of Vita Marković.

But there she was.

"Vita! Did I hurt you?" He was beside himself, scrambling to reassemble her books and tuck in the hem of his shirt, to look at her for a minute before he had to leave her for class. "I'm really sorry, Vita."

She grinned. He hadn't hurt her, and he was that same nervous boy he was when she'd talked to him at the grocery, a nervous boy who liked her. "You ever get that sugar for your mother?" she asked.

He did not understand how she could be so composed. "You'll be late, Vita. We got to go."

"Nice to see you anyway, Tony," she said, still there in front of him like she had all the time in the world and him with two flights up to get to his classroom on time.

"Come to the game tonight, Vita. I'll walk you home."

She seemed to nod. Had he seen it correctly? Flustered, he nearly bumped into a tiny girl and her friend as he climbed the stairs, seventh graders, he thought, dallying their way to someplace while he stormed past like his own fierce wind, ready to shake all the fall leaves loose and send them tumbling. He'd finally seen Vita again. Asked her to walk with him. And maybe she'd get to see him play at the game that night.

"Hey, Tony," he heard behind him. "The game don't start til seven, you know," one of his friends teased and rammed his head into Tony's shoulder. "Don't let 'em get you!"

Tony was not about to let anything get to him now until he met up with Vita after the game. He bounded into the classroom, lightheaded with the thought of her.

"You're late, Mr. Babić," his teacher pronounced as Tony took his seat. This man thought everyone was some kind of mister or miss.

"Sorry," Tony heard himself stammer, his eyes avoiding the teacher and even the classmates around him. Whoever he looked in the eye would know he wasn't sorry at all. His heart sang. He'd finally seen Vita Marković and he'd see her again.

The rest of the hours that day lumbered no matter how fast he moved, so that by the start of the game, Tony had gotten himself into a state. The coach probably wasn't going to play him. Vita would end up working in the grocery and never arrive. She'd change her mind. She'd forget—or maybe she hadn't heard him right at all. Maybe she thought they'd walk some other time.

He sat on the bench, and minutes after the game began, it started to rain. Tony hated football games in the rain. He grumbled like the other boys, but he really hated it, the way his gear slid around, the muck on his shoes, his lousy hand-me-down shoes that didn't belong on a football field and lucky he had them at all, passed on from the oldest Grillo boy out at the Morris who got them from who knew where. The grassy field got soggy. Rain glistened in the overhead lights. At half time the high school band played anyway, making a flag formation that didn't look like a flag and pounding out "You're A Grand Old Flag" in barely recognizable notes.

Running back from the locker room after half time, Tony tried to find Vita in the sea of small faces, row after row, umbrellas popped up here and there, coats held over heads. He sat on the bench in misery. He didn't like being a fool. At home, he was the eldest. He was something. Kids in the Morris Location showed respect because he was smart and played football and set an example. His teachers recognized his diligence. He stayed interested in classes, did his homework, passed his tests. He had a nice look too—he thought so anyway.

He wasn't meant to sit on a bench in the rain going crazy over a girl he hardly knew. Luka would never be in this situation. None of those Chicago cops would.

"To hell with this," Tony said aloud to himself, the rain coming harder, the score 7-22 for the other team.

"Whadya say, Ton?" His bench mate kept his eyes on the game.

"Nothing."

The boy nodded.

Six rows up in the stands behind him, Vita Marković, flanked by her girlfriends, sat wet and miserably but happily waiting for the game to end. She did not understand football, had not a clue what all the running and tackling was about. Sometimes the football sailed high above the field and was caught perfectly, and sometimes the boys fell on top of one another in a tangled, dangerous heap. The crowd roared and booed. A man's voice like that of God on high announced a play or score and all the while the rain this night continued. Vita adjusted her position in the bleachers, enduring patiently until it would end and she could walk home in the dark with Tony Babić.

She hadn't told her friends. She hadn't told anyone, just in case something went wrong or Tony changed his mind. And anyway, this secret seemed to warm her more than the two sweaters she was wearing. Like a small fire there just under the buttons of her dress.

After the game, Vita climbed down the bleachers to the edge of the football field. "Where are you going?" Kitty insisted, sick of the weather and losing besides.

"I thought I'd see the team when they came back out."

"Why?" asked Marguerite, rain dripping off her hair. "I'm going home."

"Me too. Come on, Vita. This is no time to think you're a cheerleader." The two walked some steps away from her. "We're going to get colds anyway, sitting in the rain for three hours."

They stared at one another. People passed them, umbrellas jabbed them, the rain seemed to be coming down with more ferocity. "I thought I might talk to someone." Vita shrugged.

"I'm leaving," Kitty said, too miserable to be curious about her friend's behavior. She and Marguerite walked faster and farther away from Vita. The lights overhead went dark, and the crowd noise dimmed as more people left the stadium.

Within a minute Vita stood alone near the bleachers, cold hands shoved low into her pockets. The boys had run through the gym door across the field. Now she walked the width of green turf to stand a short distance from that door, sure that the boys on the team would all crash out at any minute. Little did she know the workings of athletic teams, the fury of coaches whose players lost so shamefully, the long-winded lectures and woeful recounting.

All she knew was the late hour, her soaking clothes, and the unexpected loneliness of the football field at night. Defeated, she began the long walk home, shivering and confused by what had not happened.

At the grocery, her father stood in the doorway, smoking a cigarette. "You're late, Vita."

"The team lost," she answered, and eyes down, went upstairs to bed.

Just minutes behind her, Tony walked with Marty Stimac, neither of them in any mood to discuss the night's sad tale. The whole sorry hour the coach berated them and strategized in a steady stream of words had put a ten-foot blockade between Tony, trapped listening, and the dream of Vita he'd held to all day.

The moment they were freed, he'd bounded out the gym door with his fragment of hope that she might have stood in the rain waiting for him all that time. Instead he found the football field more deserted than he'd ever seen it.

"You think we lost cause of the rain?" Marty had asked, coming up behind him. Tony didn't answer. If he tried to talk, he thought he might cry right then and there, a football player and oldest son, with the feelings of a sad sack. That was another thing Luka would never do.

He was sure of it.

Tony was the first of Ma's kids to live,

and I'm the last.

I'm the one left to know.

I'm the one left now to know

about family

and faith

about order and want

about truth.

Johnny Babić

FAMILY

When I was a kid, Tony was the hero, the first boy, the smart one. My older sisters always said that. Tony was the smart one, my brother Pete the funny one, and me, Johnny, the charmer. That's what they always said. I could get my way with my sisters back then, tease them like to get what I wanted. We had lots of fun, all of us did, kidding around.

But what was easy? Nothing was easy. My dad came home half corned every payday, spending money we didn't have to buy whiskey or moonshine. We were kids in Prohibition, but everyone drank anyway. Cooked up their own brews. Women, too, but not my mother. Ma didn't break rules. She shuffled around and made good, that's what she did.

Petey and I were nuts about Tony. The guy did everything right. Like a hero. That's what Tony was to us, to me and Pete. He was God himself. We'd follow him all over the house, watch him shine in the neighborhood. All those kids in the Morris Location made Tony their hero too.

I don't know why. He just had that thing some guys have, a way. I mean, he was good and then he was more than good. Here was this nice-looking kid who was going to be something. He had it in him to be something. We never knew what that something would be back then. We didn't think, oh Tony will be president or run U.S. Steel. We never thought like that. Real people didn't become president. Presidents became president. But we thought a guy like my brother would go someplace, discover something, make money, rise up.

My dad was rough on me, but I never saw him rough on Tony. I had my own ideas, that's where my trouble came with the old man. I wanted a car. Pa said no car, he never drove a car. This was when I was older, maybe twelve or thirteen, and all the things with Tony had already happened. I got myself a car anyway. Hid it in the woods. But Tony kept to the straight and narrow. Maybe he had his own ideas, but I was too much a kid to notice. Me and Petey, we'd fool around, tagging after Tony like a couple of clowns. Petey was a clown, too, my brother Pete. He could make anyone laugh, flash that grin of his ear-to-ear.

I miss Pete. We weren't even two years apart. But I'll say he was in a slower lane than me. Stayed in that slower lane. Married his first girlfriend. Bought one of those small lots they were selling off for a buck over in Home Acres, put up his little house, and stayed there until he dropped. Good guy, my brother Pete. He never finished high school because he got married, but Petey was smart. Best electrician I knew.

But he wasn't smart like Tony. Tony had books. I still picture those books stacked on a chair where we ate, that area off the kitchen with a couple dozen chairs around for all of us and the boarders. Ma would say, "Tony, move, move," waving her hand at those books, hair in a babushka, apron wrapped around her. "Move, move." She was a saint, my ma, working like she did, and never mean, never hard. She knew about fifty words of English, but she'd kind of shush at us, wave her hands and we all knew what she meant. We tried to teach her, poor Ma. Keeping animals, cooking for twenty-some people, doing all that laundry and her kids going "say this word, Ma, say that word, Ma."

She'd have Tony move his books because she needed the chair, but she was proud of those books. I would see that look on her face, same as when she had a new baby. The books were from school and the library, but they were from another world too. Books were from a world where one woman didn't feed a house of people three times a day and scrub the wood floor and prime the cold pump. Books meant a different life. I saw it in her, kid that I was. She would have given those books their own chair if she'd had one to spare.

My sisters went to school, too, but not like Tony. I never saw Margaret or Anna or Katie bring home books. They were in line after Tony, one of them two years younger, one four years, one six years, then Petey eight years younger, and me just after that. Then we had two more brothers and another sister later. But the younger ones hardly knew Tony. They didn't get the chance to know him like me and Pete tugging at him and teasing like we did. Ma had four kids before Tony that didn't live long. That's what I mean, how she was a saint. She never had any help other than my older sisters. They were good, though, my sisters. Church goers all their lives. Good people. But they didn't read. They learned how to read, like I did, but the rest of us weren't readers like Tony, back and forth to the library with his books.

When Tony got a girlfriend, we didn't know. The kids in the Morris, those girls always liked Tony, I could see that. I always could see things like that. Even when I was real young, I had this way where I knew what was what. Always did and still do. Any room, any crowd, big shots and the rest, I figure them out. It's a good thing. I like people. Mostly they mean well and if they don't—busybodies, cheaters, and the like—I know it right away. Same as the sense there's a deer close by in the woods. A feel for fish under the ice. That kind of thing, you either got it or you don't.

But I never sensed Vita.

Tony just turned sixteen and football was over. Pete and me were monkeying around this day, grabbing at Tony's things, his jacket and things by the door, and out fell a note. Dear Tony, it said, then scribbled words we didn't know how to read, all those curvy letters written on the note. We knew Dear Tony though. We knew that much. We could read the four letters at the bottom too. V – I – T – A. Vita.

"Hey, Tony," I remember Petey saying loud in the kitchen, Ma at the stove, Anna setting plates around the table. "Who's Vita? Who's Vita, Tony?" Ma was over there muttering to herself in Croatian like she did when she was working, praying her rosary maybe or who knew. But Anna turned like a machine, stiff as could be.

"What Vita?" she asked, mouth kind of open. "Is that a note from Vita Marković?"

Tony had been reading one of his schoolbooks, *Our*

World's History—thick and open on his lap—fingers drumming with energy, memorizing dates in ancient time while his mother and sister got dinner, ignoring his kid brothers hopping around like jack rabbits. At Vita's name, he jerked up looking this way and that, shaking his head like he'd been swimming underwater. Then he saw Petey holding the note, unfolded in his hand. He stood and pitched toward us, all in one movement, yanked the note from Pete's hand before Petey saw it coming and grabbed my brother's shirt by the collar.

"What the hell you doing?" he swore and pinched Pete's ear, twisting it until Pete cried out in a mix of sorriness and pain. I slid away across the room and behind a chair.

"You assholes!" Tony hollered to both of us, sending my sister Anna into a tizzy about the language, Ma still muttering, closing it all out, me holding onto the chair like it's a life raft. "Mind your own business!" And there was Anna calling for Margaret and Katie to come, as if three girls could balance the odds, and Pete wailing and me cowering, Tony slamming around folding that note in his hands all careful like he's got the letter right from Jesus himself.

That's how we found out about Vita.

It was just after the first snow, all the trees stripped

bare, the raw ore of the mine dotted by white mounds, the road out front frozen for the winter. I was in the first grade and learning to spell. Now I knew V – I – T – A.

I'd seen her too. Ma took me with her to Marković's Grocery once and there was a girl, her face and hands smooth like a stone you want to keep because it feels so good to hold onto it. Vita was a pretty, pretty girl. My sisters were good looking, too, in those days, Margaret maybe the best, but they weren't what I'd call smooth. Vita was that kind of girl gets noticed. A girl you don't forget. So I knew who she was from Marković's Grocery and what she looked like and her name which I now could also spell and I knew that she wrote a note to Tony.

"She your girlfriend?" I dared to ask much later that night. "You got a girlfriend now, Tony?"

He didn't answer me. He glared and shook his head, not to say no he didn't have a girlfriend, but to say no he wasn't interested in telling a six-year-old kid brother about Vita Marković.

I didn't blame him. What the hell. We were dumb kids, like he said. We should mind our own business.

Thing is, at six like I was, and eight like Pete, you hardly got any business. We walked a mile to school and back. Slapped a rock all over the icy road with makeshift hockey sticks, goofed around the house. What was our business if it wasn't Tony and his huge life with everything from Chicago and cop letters to whiskers and thick books, football and a girlfriend? Petey and me, we couldn't get enough of Tony's business.

So maybe that's why he got all secret on us for a while. It was a lousy Christmas that year anyway. Some boarders left, like Luka had years before, not saying much of why or where. Ma was getting big with another baby, which turned out to be her last, but we didn't know that. Seemed babies kept coming and coming. That was family back then. Kids on top of kids.

Then Pa's ornery streak kicked in. He'd never say it was one thing or another, but he'd roar up like a bear in thorns. Those times Ma would kind of sink down an inch or two smaller and keep her Croatian prayers coming day and night. My older sisters ignored him. I never knew how they did that, just went on with whatever they were doing. Katie would smile all winsome, which worked most times. He'd chuckle at her then, tell her what a good girl she was. Me and Pete were that age just naturally finds trouble, leaves shoes in the way, busts a soup bowl, forgets to close the door tight and all hell would break loose. That's what

I remember of that Christmas. Maybe I got coal in my stocking, which seems to ring a bell. But don't ask me why. There probably wasn't a why.

It was the Christmas Tony got his job as a store clerk in a meat market. Back then a family would have a farm and then a store to sell their chickens and meats. This was an Italian place where I went later, but Tony worked there first. He wanted money to take Vita to the movies, Anna said. Tony always talked to Anna because that was Anna—the solid one. Margaret was the boss and Katie the sweetheart. Everyone had their place. In a big family, you get to know your place.

That job meant we didn't see Tony as much. Then pretty soon, he got back to his old self. He let us tug all over on him like always, even tease around about Vita. He'd swat at us and tease back. Called us the Kid Geniuses. That was his name for us then because it was so far from true. "Tony's in love," we'd chant and he'd grin like this was so and he was proud it was. Katie told us she'd seen Tony and Vita holding hands after school.

I liked thinking about this. My brother and pretty Vita Marković holding hands and going to movies. "You think they kiss?" I asked Pete, which sent him into a fit of goofball faces. My brother Pete was a funny, funny guy. He'd pick up a broom and pretend it was a guitar or tip an empty milk bottle into his mouth and stagger around like he was drunk. The kind of stuff that always made me laugh, made all of us laugh.

What did we know?

TWO

Spring and Summer 1928

i.

Men sat in those plain rooms, heads bent to one another, bald or groomed, wire-rimmed glasses rubbed clean by the white hand-kerchiefs folded in their pockets. Most wore ties. One of their own preferred a dapper bow, but all shared a purpose—to tame the wild streets of Prohibition, streets the city no longer con-trolled and had not controlled for years. This fact continued to dog certain powers of Chicago, the ranks of clean cops and those who led the clean cops—those not part of the brotherhood of crime—who wanted to be in charge, but mostly were not.

These managers in the city of Chicago had their high-level rank and pay and lived on the North Side with wives who did good deeds in the morning and played bridge in the afternoons. Their children remained well-behaved and reasonably superior, but the men were not effectual. The whole lawless power of gangsters from Sicily and then New York, even from out in the suburbs now, did as they pleased, willing to break the arms and legs of those who did not vote the way they wanted them to vote.

It was a serious time. Beads of sweat broke out on the faces of these men even in the most bitter of snowstorms, the most chilling of late rains. Even at home in their armchairs reading the *Tribune* headlines—*Police Kill Outlaw in Gun Battle – Aiello Foes Shot from Ambush – Alcohol Feud Flares Up at Death Corner*—they felt the fear of their circumstances, the edge where they perched. It didn't end.

Capone's organization wasn't alone on the South Side. In this part of town where most of Chicago's Black people lived, a separate crime world existed, equally dangerous and thriving. Luca didn't cover those neighborhoods, but he'd followed his buddies to the jazz clubs on two occasions, intrigued by Black and white couples, the dancing, the thrill of a music he had never heard before. Patrons kept their flasks hidden, he supposed, and he hadn't come to the clubs to judge anyway. "We're off duty here," one of his fellows had repeated as he sat mesmerized, slapping his knee to the beat. The South Side had its own aldermen and lawyers, and its own Black crime bosses who did not meddle with the Italians nor with the Irish of the North Side. And they expected the same in return.

For cops anywhere out on the street, the fight of good against evil mounted and remained complicated. Some cops were on the take. Some were dangerous to know. Others would step in front of you to take the first bullet. None of this was myth or tall tale. It was life in Chicago.

Luka's faith in his work had not wavered, though he now wrote fewer letters to his mother back home and fewer letters to Tony

Babić in Minnesota. He drank more, lots of godawful stuff brewed by his Irish buddies and their devoted uncles, cousins, and dads. Every day there was something to decide, something that had to do with goodness—because all around was the opposite of that. He found a Croatian church on East Ninety-Sixth Street and took the train there every Sunday. The Franciscan friars comforted him, as did the parish ladies serving up coffee and sweet povitica after Mass. Here were people who sounded like home, and Luka put extra coins in the collection plate to feel that he belonged. The parish wanted to build a school, remodel the old rectory, that's what they were thinking about. They were not wondering if they would be shot in the street.

Luka hated the mayor, William Hale Thompson, who had taken office for his second time the year before. He was a close ally of mob boss Al Capone and a cocky, corrupt man. Big Bill, as he was known—as if he were a pal out in the great Wild West—had lost some of his clout in the Republican primary that week, a free for all kind of event that the police department could not contain. Politicians and voters on both sides threw hand grenades at one another like penny candy at a parade. Luka had never been so frightened in his life, not even when he'd traveled to America in a ship that listed near sideways in the middle of an Atlantic storm.

He'd come back to his apartment that April day of the primary and put on the sweater his older sister had knit for him before he left home. Her stitches were so even, so close, a labor of love, he thought, pulling it around him for comfort. His sister would not believe the stories he now could tell her, and if he were back there in that Croatian village, he would not believe them either—that a guy named Big Bill could be mayor of a city like Chicago and in the grip of a maniac like Al Capone. Luka wished he had not seen and heard the goings on at that Republican primary, the hate on men's faces, the determination to do damage all around. More than one grenade had exploded within feet of Luka and he hadn't been able to stop them. He became a cop to fight crime, not to stand in the middle of crime pointing his gun at a mob that did not care what he said or did. He wasn't the kind of cop who loved his own power. But he hadn't planned on having no power either.

The newspaper the next day announced that Thompson had been crushed in the ward fight, but Luka was not fool enough to suppose the mayor would fade away. In fact, Thompson told the world it was ridiculous for him to step down. And then over the next months the gang activity grew oddly quiet. Word on the street was they were pledging a sort of peace until after the presidential election, an arrangement had been made among the mayor, Capone, and the New York mob bosses. That was the word. And maybe it was so.

In the heat of that summer the men who wanted a better Chicago almost relaxed. People focused on the presidential election, on the Cubs, the White Sox, on any breeze they could catch off Lake Michigan. Luka wrote to Tony Babić that he was remembering their visit of the year before and what was Tony up to these days. I'm still fighting crime here, Luka said. Say hi to your mother. Tell her how much I miss her fresh baked bread.

Not two weeks later, Luka heard back from Tony. The boy was a clerk in a meat market now, had been working there since December. He had a girlfriend named Vita. He never thought he'd ever have a girlfriend as pretty as Vita, Tony wrote, and he hoped that Luka could meet her someday soon. Maybe Luka would come visit them all. Maybe Luka had a girlfriend too.

But Luka did not have a girlfriend to write about, though he'd met a girl at church he would talk with after Mass. She always wore a close-fitting hat that he thought might be the style just then, pale pink with a wide ribbon of the same color wrapped round. When she looked at him, it seemed she was peeking out from under a mound of frosting. But he didn't tell her that. They talked about the old country and who they'd left behind, and then they'd talk about what each of them planned to do that day. This girl, her name was Kata, liked to window shop on Sunday, she said. He'd never heard that term, window shop. How would a young man from a remote Croatian village who had worked as a miner and a street cop ever know about such a thing as window shopping? He got the feeling that Kata enjoyed life, that she didn't need too much going her way to count a day good and satisfying. She worked as a telephone operator, her English exceptional, he noted, and she said this was because all her life she had wanted to come to America and speak like a citizen and dress like a lady.

"How about you, Luka?" she asked often. She wanted to know about his own ambitions, what had brought him to his current life and why and where it might lead. But after a short hour, Kata would shake his hand, her glove smooth in his grip, and leave for her wanders about the city, her window shopping, as she said.

On September 7th that year, Al Capone's friend and adviser Tony Lombardo was gunned down on a busy intersection during rush hour. Luka wasn't there, but other cops talked about it for weeks. The way the people of Chicago, going home from work and minding their own business, were suddenly pushing this way and that, not knowing where the bullets were coming from or for whom they were intended, shopkeepers running into the street to see what was happening, then hurrying back inside to lock their doors. The gunmen came from behind and shot Lombardo in the head, his bodyguard in the back, another bodyguard wounded but not dead, unwilling to talk. "Hoffman says, who shot you, says it to him in Italian. You're going to die anyway, he says. Who shot you? And you think he gets an answer?" That's what Luka's friend Danny Cox said to him. Danny had been right there, saw Lombardo go down, saw the chaos and heard about the Assistant State Attorney Sam Hoffman, trying to get information out of the bodyguard who survived. "He's going to die anyhow," Danny repeated. "What's he holding out for? These guys are as dumb as they are nuts."

Luka had nodded as if he agreed. But he wasn't sure he thought the gangsters were dumb.

"The shooters weren't from Chicago though, right, Danny?"

"New York guys after Capone is what I hear. But they're dead too. Maybe shot by their own, maybe shot by Capone." Danny scrambled the curls on his head with large, rough hands. "Dead is dead."

The Chicago Tribune reported that Lombardo's wife was home making dinner, wearing her housedress, her kids in the yard playing. That was something Luka tried to understand. That these guys, these violent guys who made money in bribes and gambling, bootlegging and women, went home to wives who raised small children and wore housedresses. It just wasn't something he could picture. It just didn't fit the picture.

ii.

Vita loved writing notes to Tony and slipping them into his hand as they passed in the school hallways, like a dream come true, this private thing between them. She loved just thinking of it, thinking about Tony and him thinking about her. She'd write in a kind of code, say things like "my best friend told me you're handsome," but not say her best friend's name or put Tony's name on the note or her own name ever, ever.

Teachers tended to be strict about notes in school, for what reason Vita did not understand. Weren't you using grammar and penmanship, weren't you thinking and creating and connecting? "It's distracting, that's why," Kitty said. "What if everyone were writing and passing notes all day? Who would learn anything?" Kitty rarely wrote notes. Her penmanship was messy, for one thing, and she didn't like how much time it took to put words on paper when you could talk to someone and be done in seconds. You could get an immediate response. And see a face and have the other person see you too, maybe wearing your new lace-trimmed collar that day. "Think of it, Vita. Notes here, there, and everywhere."

"You don't understand," was all Vita had in answer.

She'd written her first note to Tony Babić just a month after the ill-fated football game in the fall. Now it was May, school almost over, and Vita estimated she'd written at least two dozen notes to Tony. At least that. In between the first note and the one she carried in her skirt pocket to give to him that day, Tony had walked her home from school about once a week, making it maybe twenty-five walks together, her elbow knocking into his, their steps in sync. He'd brushed snow off her hat, held an umbrella over her head, and lifted her, however briefly, over a snowbank back in January.

She took it all to heart. They'd gone to two movies together— one with Charlie Chaplin and one with Buster Keaton. In the elegant darkness of the State Theater side balcony, he'd held her hand, near for dear life, she thought, his grip strong, his pulse racing.

In the beginning, they'd talked about school and goings on in town, about their childhood escapades and games. Both remembered the town moving, knew the stories. Men showing up on their lunch breaks to move their families from north to south in one hour, everyone in turmoil. Graves opened in the old cemetery to reveal the dead who had awakened in their boxes, buried alive in some unconscious state, fingers clawed to the bone in their efforts to escape.

They had both heard of the two-story house en route to its lot in the Alice Addition, rolling along with horses, logs, tractors, steam crawlers, and cables the way everything was moved, until something went awry, and the house collapsed to near twigs right there on Third Avenue. Or the one about the lady who went into labor in the old part of town and gave birth in the new. Those were the stories that claimed their commonality, the town they knew, the history shared.

Then after a while, midwinter it was, they talked more about themselves, starting at the outer edges, what it was like working as clerks in stores, the customers who came and went at Marković's and the Italian meat market where Tony put in afterschool shifts and all day Saturday. They talked about kids coming in with lists their mothers had written in broken English, spreg chik and the like. They talked about the serious shoppers who wanted only today's eggs, today's butter, the bone cut of meat. They had these grown-up conversations, the larger world of commerce and all.

When they were sitting across from each other—in the school library or cafeteria—they'd study one another, held by every word and gesture. So Vita knew the exact shade of Tony's eyes, a gray-green-sometimes-blue color that she found almost transparent, unsettling in their luminosity. Not that her thoughts used such words. Her thoughts avoided words. Her thoughts were images of Tony beside her, with her, maybe forever.

When they walked side by side, it was a different experience. They were making their way together, trudging across snowy mounds of ore, heads into gales of wind, whipped by rain, sometimes guided by night stars. These were the images in Vita's mind, thoughts that needed no words, visions of a life she thought she favored. She and Tony against the world.

Now they were nearing something else. Away from others, Tony put his arm around her waist, his hand circling around to the front of her body, not there but almost there. It terrified her how light-headed she'd feel when that happened, how she longed for something she could not name and this dissolution of strength, her legs barely able to hold her as they walked along. They talked mindlessly at those moments. They'd say anything—that Tony needed to clean his boots for work in the market or when Vita would finish her math equations, the strange cloud up ahead, the cold air anything—anything but his hand wrapped around her waist to the front of her body.

When they weren't so physically close, their conversations made way for more silence. They settled into quiet together in a comfort neither of them had known with anyone outside their families. And then Tony might break the silence by speculating on his future, recalling the cops in Chicago, wondering about the mines. Vita shared her confusion about the options for girls. Would she always work for her family in the store? Should she learn shorthand to be in an office someplace? The mining company had an office, didn't it?

They would not talk about a future together, though they both dreamed some version of this, vague dreams that came in a moment and quickly darted off like nervous little sparrows. Neither of them had older siblings or friends who had already chosen a partner for life. It wasn't an easy conjecture just then. They didn't make a show of their attachment. It wasn't in their natures. And it wasn't wise.

Vita's parents had old country ways and Tony's father was cautious of his position in town. They might all be pioneers, but they were Eastern Europeans with only their hard work and reputations to protect them. That was true for both families. Each in its way. The mothers were friends. The fathers knew one another slightly and neither was prepared to have a son or daughter wasting time on the nonsense of young love. If you were going to marry, then that's what you did. You didn't fool around in the dark without purpose. You worked hard and raised a family. In the world of immigrant fathers, life was a serious business.

At school, Vita kept her notes and Tony's in the pocket of her skirt. Nowhere else. At home, she had cleaned out a spice tin with a lid. She tucked the notes inside. Then she folded her underwear and extra stockings on top of it. She didn't think anyone in her family would find them hidden there, though she shared her small bedroom with her older sister who did tend to be on alert about most everything. But this scheme was the best she could devise. Tony's notes were a treasure to her and nothing she would ever throw away or destroy. She couldn't bear to think of it.

"Where do you keep my notes to you, Tony?"

She'd asked this several times, thinking he may have a strategy that was better than hers. But he'd answered that it was a secret. "Even from me?" She didn't think he should have secrets from her. Not really. Not anymore.

In truth, Tony did not keep her notes beyond a day or two. The entire enterprise of the notes felt too risky to him living in a house with three sisters and four little brothers. After he'd read Vita's notes over and over such that he could remember almost all the words she'd written, he would drop them into his mother's stove and let them burn to sweet hot ash.

"They're where nobody will find them, Vita."

"I can't imagine where though," she answered.

And he let it go at that.

iii.

Tony had no experience of Bennet Park like Vita did. His social life happened at school or in the Morris Location. The park was another world. "You've never heard the City Band?" She had been incredulous and talked about the park all through winter and early spring. The shelter of the pavilion and the buzz of the community. All the kids who hung around there in the summer. She loved the music—"Yankee Doodle Dandy" and "Ol' Man River"—however out of tune. That was Vita. Looking for the charm, being part of the crowd.

As soon as school ended, they made a plan to go to the park together. "We'll have such a good time, Tony," she said, and he could not resist her.

But he also could not explain, even to himself, how uneasy he felt. "Where you going, Tony?" His younger brothers kept nagging. "Why you wearing a tie, Tony? You going out with Vita? Where you going anyway?" His sister Katie hovered, grinning like she knew the secret, and Anna watched him all day wondering why he was fussing so much with his hair, worrying about his tie, as though he were off to meet the Pope in Rome instead of Vita Marković. But she said nothing. And finally he felt he looked as good as he could for Bennet Park, a place that in his mind represented the town at large, outside his realm, a place where school friends might congregate but without the context of school, without the expectations of a school day or a school team. It wasn't his world.

He hurried to town, trying to not sweat, to remain in charge of himself. At Marković's Grocery, he joked with Vita's brother, Billy, before holding the door for Vita, who wore her light brown dress with a straw hat trimmed by a ribbon. "You look great," he said, working to sound smooth and contained. "Really great, Vita."

They walked holding hands and entered the park alongside the golf course still holding hands. The band was playing, as she'd said it would be, but he didn't like how it sounded. Out at the Morris they had a neighbor, Sonny Stimac, who played accordion ten times better, a mellow layered sound Sonny played that settled on the air real easy. Not this band's mix of instruments half out of tune and out of sync. Tony recognized lots of the guys on the ball field, but that tugged at him, too, guys from his football team out there without him. Vita waved at people, called out to girls she knew as they made their way, her wide hat sliding around on her pretty head. Nobody called out to him, although he also knew people. They certainly noticed him with Vita and he was sure he looked presentable—or better than presentable—but here in town he was not Tony Babić the star that he was out at the

Morris Location. He smiled anyway, tried not to reveal himself. Tried to remember that just a little over a mile away he was a guy who belonged.

Vita asked him to push her on a swing, which he did and then he sat on a swing next to her, winding the chains until they were tight and letting them go into a fast twirl the way she did, and there they were, Vita laughing, holding on to the brim of her hat. It was just past sunset and without saying or agreeing, the two of them moved over to the picnic tables near the pavilion. Old oaks and pines blocked most of the park from view, though the band played on and on, its tinny notes carrying across to them. Tony climbed onto a table to sit and pulled Vita close to him. He let the feelings of the night take over, his worries and estrangement, the dark and nearly crazed attraction for Vita in his arms. Whatever happened, he couldn't think later, couldn't remember, for it was like a wave, like the most fierce wave off that lake in Chicago and it rushed over him and he held on to Vita and she held on to him and there was nothing but the two of them on a table in the park she had always said he would love the way that she did.

This was the moment. Beyond all their other moments together, he and Vita, this was the moment that Tony wanted her for the rest of his life, for his own, and this moment came in a rushed and circled haze. She had a scent, an orange kind of scent, and a solid body, like he'd never known, not hard and not soft. Something new, all hers, all his. Maybe she would go home and remember every move, but walking back around the mine later that night,

Tony did not. Only sensations, like shooting stars in the night, like falling stars.

He didn't dream. He barely slept. The park spread out before him, a vision, a strange land where he went with Vita Marković and the music fell away and so did all the people playing ball and milling around in groups he knew or never knew, and it was just him and Vita riding on a picnic table near the pines waiting for the earth to stop spinning.

iv.

Kitty was at the store first thing, wiggling a finger for Vita to come outside with her. "Tell me everything," she said as soon as they crossed to the opposite boulevard. "I saw you leave the park with Tony. So where did you go? What happened?"

"We didn't leave the park."

"But I didn't see you."

"We went up by the pavilion and sat on a picnic table."

"There has to be more to the story, Vita. You finally got Tony Babić to the park and then you both disappeared. There has to be a story."

Of course there was a story. But not a story to tell Kitty, not a girlfriend story. What had happened for Vita was a mystery, a crossing into a mysterious place with Tony and the night. She did not want to say. She could not say.

"Vita?" Kitty sat down on the grass and pulled out a dandelion turned white with fluff and seed. "Fine then, I'll tell you about my night, since you'll never ask. Marguerite had some business at home, an uncle from Germany or somebody, so I asked my cousin Mikey to go with me and he said sure and then when we got there he started talking to Frank Macchi—you know with the curly hair—and then we all watched the ball game together. And I sat in the middle." She beamed her triumph. "Between them."

"That's nice, Kitty."

"Nice is when the sun shines, Vita. Sitting between two boys at a ballgame is—I don't know—it's great. Everyone saw us." She searched Vita's face for acknowledgment. "That's what I think, anyway. I think it's great."

Vita nodded and smiled at her friend, her best friend, all high and happy over her moment with two boys at the park, even though one was her cousin Mikey and she'd invited him herself. But Vita didn't feel any thrill for Kitty, as she might have at one time. At some time. At a time when any brush with boys was worthy and breathtaking. A time before Tony Babić's skin against her skin and his mouth open on her own and his heat her heat and their heat consuming.

"Do you like Frank Macchi then?"

Kitty squinted, narrowing her focus on Vita. "Of course! Why do you think I'm telling you this story? At least I know what is a story and am willing to share it with my friends." She paused, hoping it would be the opening where Vita relayed the details of her night with Tony on a picnic table in an unseen part of Bennet Park. But that did not happen. Vita continued to sit across from Kitty, but at least fifty miles away, someplace near the Canadian border where the trees grew so thick it would be hard to know where you were. That was Vita this morning. In her mysterious land, she had left Kitty behind, cross-legged on the ground, Kitty's skirt tucked around her, hair bobbed in that way she'd seen in a newsreel—and alone. She'd left poor Kitty alone.

"I better go help my mom," Vita said, rising and swishing away the bits and pieces of the ground on her dress. "You know," she added by way of some explanation. "There's so much to do in the mornings."

But Kitty did not answer. She waved and remained where she sat, snatching dandelions and blowing their feathery pods away, the June morning light on her dark hair and the simple houses of their Brooklyn neighborhood in formation behind her.

"Want to talk later, Kitty?" Vita asked. "I'll come over. We could go looking for strawberries. That's always fun," Vita added, though it was clear that picking strawberries on the edges of the ore dumps would not make up for her lack of confidence in her friend, for the absolute fact that she had chosen Tony Babić over Kitty now and was not about to relinquish that allegiance for any good times of old.

Still, both Kitty and Vita loved wild strawberries.

That was one thing they had together.

v.

Tony could not hide his distraction. He had never known this, this jittery lack of concentration. His mother hollering his name to get him out of her way as he stood lost in the middle of the room. Mrs. Conti's "Eh, Tony, *fai attenzione*, you," as he stared vacantly at the shadows shifting on the walls of the meat market. In the neighborhood, he held to the sidelines, encouraging his friends, nodding like an old uncle, but not crashing to the middle. Not grabbing the ball or kidding with them. He watched. He smiled.

Nobody could possibly know the kind of feeling he had for Vita, the significance. In his mind Tony called it love, saw the word love before him and felt its heartbeat, the moist, enormous connection of love. His parents married to come to this country and though they had one baby after another, which took some kind of making, a physical togetherness, he did not believe they had the fever and intensity for each other that he had for Vita. Jocco had never lost track of reality in his life. Of this, Tony was certain.

"Come play catch with us," his younger brothers begged. It was

Sunday. They'd marched to church and back like God's army and were waiting for their mother and sisters to deliver the noon meal. Low endless clouds hung white and loose. He didn't have to work and he was taking Vita to a movie that night. He tossed the ball first to Pete, then Johnny, enjoying their antics—tripping each other and giggling, yet throwing mighty throws.

"You two are athletes," Tony called across the space between them. "Small-town heroes, that's what you're going to be."

"No, you, Tony," Pete yelled back.

"Tony's in love, aren't ya, Tony?" Johnny grinned at him like a mystic.

"You know nothing," Pete argued and wrestled the ball away from him. "Right, Tony?"

But Tony had no answer. His kid brother Johnny never missed a beat, an interaction, or a mood shift. So, of course, Johnny could see that his older brother's mind was not on throwing the ball or sitting at the table with kids and boarders. It was over at Markovič's Grocery, behind the counter with a pretty girl in a light brown dress.

When Tony got there to pick up Vita hours later, it wasn't her brother, Billy, working the store or any of her sisters or her mother who was friends with Tony's mother. It was Vita's dad. Tony had never met Vita's dad before. He was a man who had left the security of his mining job to run a grocery store. He was not about any foolishness, this man, and coming into the store and meeting his eyes, Tony could see that. George Marković reminded him of mother raccoons he'd encountered in the woods on the far side of the Morris, those same fierce eyes.

Tony took tentative steps inside. "Hi, Mr. Marković. I'm Tony Babić," he said. "I'm here to pick up Vita."

The older man gave a nod. But he didn't move to call his daughter or to greet her suitor. He sat on his stool and watched Tony watching him. "Where you going?"

"To see a movie."

"What's that like?"

"A movie?"

Mr. Marković nodded again.

Tony had to think. "It's watching a story with real people, but on a flat screen, like a curtain. Mostly they're silent movies. But sometimes they talk and sing."

"Pretty dark."

"Inside? The place is a little dark, but they have lights too. In the corners and over doors. So it's safe."

Mr. Marković took this in and then laughed, deeply but without merriment. Jocco laughed like that all the time. It made Tony nervous, the lack of humor in that kind of laugh. "How about you, kid? Are you safe?" He turned away from Tony and called upstairs to Vita.

Then he said, "I don't favor this," to Tony, who continued to stand just inside the store, in the exact spot he'd found for himself the minute he'd entered, a square foot of worn wood where he'd planted his feet and forgotten to move them. He was not sure what to say. Maybe Vita's father did not know about their other dates or walks around town. Maybe her mother and siblings had kept this information a secret, allowing Tony to fall in love with a girl whose father didn't know he existed.

"You Jocco's boy?"

"Yes, sir," Tony answered.

"Nobody messes with Jocco Babić. Did you know that?"

Tony shook his head. He only wanted to do and say whatever this man wanted or expected him to do and say. Not one thing more or less.

"I'm the same. Jocco and me, we're the same," Mr. Marković added. That's when Vita appeared at the foot of the stairs from the apartment where the family lived.

"Hi, Tony." She did not smile or reach out. Her arms were close around her, holding onto a little purse she had sewn for herself, and her focus was on her father not Tony. "I'll be back soon, Pa. Don't worry." Then she hurried out as though to stay ahead of trouble.

She waved at her father and almost ran around the corner to be out of his sight.

Tony was shaken. "He doesn't know about me! You didn't tell him. Now I show up and it's like I'm a criminal come to steal his daughter."

"Well, he did let me go."

"Let you go? We just ran out the door!"

"He doesn't think girls should go out until they're ready to get married."

"How do you know you're ready to get married if you never go out with someone?"

"I don't know what he thinks about, Tony. Maybe he thinks it just happens."

Tony kicked the grit on the shoulder of the road. "Well, this is happening."

Vita tried to soothe him, though the encounter had upset her as much as it did him. Her father had laid down his rules years ago and now Vita was going against them. But her mother liked the Babić family and knew that lots of respectable girls went with boys, that they walked with boys and went to movies and dances with boys. That was why she'd kept Vita's relationship with Tony from her husband and why all Vita's siblings had as well. Vita's mother considered herself modern. She tried to be anyway.

And George Marković had a life of his own in the world, sourcing food for the store, drinking in the kitchens of his Croatian friends, and working on the grocery's finances at his table in the back room, shelves of staples stacked around him. His eyes weren't on the every move of his wife and kids. His eyes were on life itself, on the numbers, the risks, the threats. That's why he didn't know about Tony Babić. His whole family had feared that he'd regard Tony as just one of those threats.

"It's the twentieth century, for God's sake," Tony grumbled, worried to his core that this man would take Vita away from him.

"Does your father let your sisters go out, Tony?"

"He keeps a gun by the door."

"A gun! What does that mean?"

They were crossing the railroad tracks that separated Park Addition from downtown and Tony stopped to face her. "We have boarders, Vita. Some are nice and maybe some aren't so nice. That's Pa's warning. That's Pa's way of saying to stay away from his daughters."

He could see that Vita was stunned. Her father might glower over the counter, but was Tony's going to shoot anyone who crossed the line? "So do your sisters go out with boys their own age?"

"Maybe when they get older."

"My mother likes you a lot, Tony."

"I like your whole family," he answered.

"Do you like my dad?"

They were almost to the movie theater by then and he glanced over to see that she was teasing him. "Sure, Vita. I can hardly wait for him to tear me to pieces and throw me to the wolves." She laughed. She wanted to hope it was all in fun and that her father would not stand in her way.

George Marković had been lucky with his kids, all of them. They minded what he said, worked hard in the store, helped their mother. Running a business, you needed no shame, that was his thinking. No upsets or bad behaviors, nothing that would push customers toward one of the other groceries all over, on half the corners of the town, family stores like his own, all with something to offer. George had worked hard for more than twenty years to stay ahead and he didn't want Vita to upend any part of his success by traipsing around town with a boy from one of the mining locations. He didn't want people talking about his daughter and Tony Babić, no matter how tough Jocco was or feared or accepted. If Vita were Jocco's girl, no boy would be within ten feet of her. Movies. What the hell were movies?

"Heh, George. Got some of that sausage of yours?"

He weighed out two pounds for his neighbor Vince Sorci. They talked about the good spell of weather, their gardens. George didn't recall half what he said to his customers. They smoked a cigarette each and chuckled about this or that.

Others came and went that night, and George Marković tended to them all, refused help from his kids and wife. He wanted to know the minute Vita arrived and he wanted to see for himself how she acted around this Tony after sitting in a dark movie the-ater with him. He wanted to see for himself.

Two hours passed. Outside the store bugs fried against the street-light and moths hovered. Finally, at 9:27 on the clock hanging above him, Vita came into the store so quietly, George almost missed the moment. "Where's that boy?"

"Oh," Vita nearly whispered, "he just walked me to the door and headed home. He has to work tomorrow." Her voice remained so soft he could barely hear her. "Do you want me to close up for you, Pa?" She spoke as though they were in a room of sick people. Or sleeping children.

He couldn't answer. Just then, watching Vita tiptoe to the door-way that led upstairs, there was nothing he could think to say.

The next day George Marković told his wife he did not want Vita spending time alone with Tony Babić. "Do you understand?" he said in that way men said such things to stress their importance.

"He's a nice boy, George. It's not the old country, you know."

He had not expected her to argue with him when he'd made himself so clear. "You heard what I said." He turned then and walked away to sit at his rickety table in the back room and count money. Behind him his wife looked across the store at her son, Billy, and shrugged. Billy shook his head. In a year or two he planned to ask girls to the movies, too, and he already had an idea of which girls he'd choose.

Even so, a line had been drawn, hard fact or fiction. A line had been drawn.

FAITH

You think everyone wants respectability, but some could care less. Riff raff's everywhere—rundown houses and yards of junk, you could make a list a mile long of bad behaviors or tendencies in that direction. In a big family, you see lots of it one way or the other. Drinking, womanizing, tempers, divorces for sure and on like that. I can't say I set out to be the most respectable guy, I liked my fun, but I must have had the idea back then, even young Johnny Babić, to keep it on the up and up. Never drank sloppy drunk, never ran around with women, none of that.

I've lived in this town all my life outside those war years, and I've made friends from the dumbest guys around to the bigshots at U.S. Steel that played golf with me right up until they all died. I had a great time with those guys and the guys I hunted and fished with, guys from work, all of them. I kept on terms with cops and schoolteachers. My lawyer here, I just drop in and have a chat with him now and then. How you doing, that kind of thing. I say hi to everyone who passes by, even the drug dealer across the street. I don't want trouble with anyone and that's the way I've always been.

I tried not to think about Tony. What was the point? And now, all these years later and everyone gone, I wonder did I stay inside the lines because of him? Prove some family respectability? My sister Margaret hung onto Jesus, Anna took care of her kids like a saint, Katie was a saint herself, but she didn't have an easy time with her husbands. And divorce back then was some kind of high crime in the church. Bunch of baloney. Nikko and Georgie had their troubles too.

Me, I stuck to music. I loved to dance and still do. I went for music and I went for dancing. Even now, I glide around that floor, dip and turn. Tommy Dorsey, Harry James, Benny Goodman, that's my music. That's what kept me right. Not many women can dance the way I dance, especially these days. My wife never was much of a dancer, but we did our best. My lady friend now, she's stiff as a board. I say loosen up, bend your knees, follow, follow. But she's not much one for following. Maybe that's the problem all around. Nobody wants to follow.

I got my music playing this minute. My kids buy me

these discs. Best of the war years, best of Frank Sinatra, Dean Martin, best of the best. I've got stacks of them.

I'll say another thing. More or less, I stayed with the church. Never cared for the sermons or all that bullshit about divorce, but I got some feeling from it, even when I was small. One time I walked alone around the Hull Rust to church and Sunday school. It was what I wanted to do and I don't know why I went alone, but that's what happened. It was cold. That sharp kind of cold we get up here, sometimes thirty below. Nothing to mess with. I told Ma, who loved her God, that I was going and she gave me an extra scarf and off I went. But coming back, my feet got so cold, I couldn't feel them. I was maybe eight, nine years old then and who knows why I was all by myself to church that Sunday. But I'll never forget it. First house at Morris, I went to the door. We knew each other, all of us. Mrs. Sabin came to the door, I'll never forget, and she hurried me inside to a chair, had me soak my feet in a tub of warm water, rubbing them for me easy like until I could feel my toes again. Then she sent me home.

My mother was wild as she could be. I'd been gone too long, the winds outside howling. My dad blamed her for Johnny going to church, but it was me chose to go. I was the one wanted to go. Some mornings now, if I've got nothing to do, I drive to church for that daily Mass, sit where I always sit, take the Communion and go home. I'm not one to give lots of money or butter up to the priests or sit there in front like I own the place. I keep to the sides. Sing if I feel like it. But I go.

First year I was in the army, the 719th Train Battalion it was, we were in North Africa making our way north, sleeping in tents, keeping the trains moving, and I got meningitis. The officers didn't know, the only medical guy we had was a dentist from New Jersey who thought it was the flu or something, so it took a few days to catch on to how sick I was. They hauled me to a hospital, put me in quarantine, and sent a telegram to my mother saying we do not think your son will make it. That's when my sisters went to church to pray for me. Every day they took to their knees to save me. However many novenas they prayed, all of them praying, it worked. Not two weeks later my mother got a letter from the war department saying that I was getting better and then another letter a week later saying Dear Mrs. Babić, I am pleased to inform you that your son was released from the hospital. I still have the letters, which is how I know what they said. Very truly yours, Major General So and So.

All my life I tell that story and people say, Johnny, it's a miracle. Back in 1943, I almost died in a tent in North Africa and here I am alive today. Maybe that's a miracle. Maybe it is. Then you got to wonder what is the opposite of a miracle? What is it when you don't pull through?

What do they call that?

THREE

Late Summer and Fall 1928

i.

In mid-October, just weeks after the Lombardo killing, Luka was assigned security for New York's Governor Al Smith, in town on his bid to be president. Chicago put forth their best for the Democratic hopeful, planning an afternoon tour of all the city's parks where regular folks could gather to see Al, as the world loved to call him, and wave and blow kisses his way.

"Load of crap, if you ask me," a cop known as Fitzy griped to Luka. "How big a deal is this getting him all over the city full of mobs and full-scale lunatics."

"He's running for president, Fitz. We do what we do." Luka hated whining. "Did you know Al Smith never went to high school? Governor of New York and he never even went to high school."

"There you go. Half the force could be president," Fitzy joked.

Hours later, after the security team had escorted Governor Smith around the city and dropped him off at the Congress Hotel where he was to rest before speaking that night at the armory, the cops took their break too—at the same café where Luka had taken Tony Babić the year before. At that time, Luka had been less sure about the undercurrents of corruption on the force, the eyes averted and money slipped into pockets. "Nothing we can do about it," he'd heard guys say. "Might as well make a few bucks." But since then he'd come to know that what happened between the cops and the bootleggers was something more than a few bucks.

Luka himself was a good cop. An honest, if sometimes brooding cop, who held no allegiances to pals he'd grown up with, or an Irish clan, or a pack of buddies from the neighborhood. Even so, the others talked in front of him, proud to brag about the big wins, the larger stashes of money made by simply looking the other way or warning speakeasies when the Feds were coming.

"Prohibition is bullshit, Luka, and you know it." That's what his friend Danny Cox had told him just months before. "Everyone drinks. You, me, the world, you name it, who don't drink?"

There was no argument to this. In the old country, his mother had a saying something like it's the chicken or it's the egg. Did they have gangs because the law made something perfectly normal into a crime, or did they have Prohibition because crime was out of hand in the first place? These were things Luka bothered over all the time. In his four years on the force, he'd seen Capone's South Side Gang grow in number and influence while cops he worked with stepped out of the way and let it happen. The mayor, the chief of police, one after the other, condemned rampant crime, but rode right alongside it anyway.

"Those guys over there," Danny had said pointing to a table of cocky, happy-go-lucky cops in the restaurant where they sat for lunch. "Those guys make over sixty thousand a year."

"I don't believe you." Luka made $3,800 and called it lucky.

"Some guys make more, Luka, that's what I'm telling you. What the hell. Capone makes millions. Why not let him share a little of that with the hardworking cops of Chicago? Right? You can hang on to your righteousness if you want, Luka, but life roars on, my lad. That's what I'm telling you."

Since that conversation he'd heard some cop boasting that he made enough to buy a yacht and cruise Lake Michigan. And "two hundred grand." He'd heard that as well. Two hundred grand. It was unthinkable. "Careful, Luka, you stay clean and broke and they'll pull you off the street for backward behavior," one of the guys said teasing.

"Don't worry about me," he answered in defense.

Luka sent Tony Babić a postcard of the North Avenue Beach on an autumn afternoon with people roaming about and the true blue of Lake Michigan stretching wide across the photo. Greetings to your family, Tony, he wrote. How's school? Keep in touch.

On November 6th, the good Governor Al Smith of New York lost the presidential election to Herbert Hoover. The Republicans rejoiced, Chicago fans of the Democratic candidate fumed, and Al Capone, in his large hats and pale-colored suits, continued to rule Chicago.

ii.

Vita had never been a rebel, not even in the frivolous way of her friend Kitty, who paid little attention to the rules of the game no matter where she was—or even in the oblivious way of Marguerite, who didn't notice or remember whatever boundaries went up around her. George Marković's decree that she was not to see Tony ripped into Vita's easy-going nature. That kind of rule was impossible, like saying she should not eat or sleep again. She was not going to live without Tony, not now, when they were so star-crossed and right.

Her father said nothing to her about it. Her mother had stumbled through the news the morning after Vita's movie date. "Be careful," her mother had concluded. Not saying she must absolutely stop seeing Tony, Vita understood. But not to have Tony come to the store, not to be obvious. Her mother's eyes had met hers woman to woman, Vita thought. A new bond of some kind. Certainly, a sympathy.

She wrote a note to Tony explaining this development and asked her brother to take it out to the Morris Location for her.

"I've never been to the Morris Location."

"It's just a place, Billy. You've got friends from school out there, I know you do."

"You want me to knock on the door?"

"Just say you're my brother. Say hello, Mrs. Babić. My sister, Vita Marković sends this letter for Tony." She folded the envelope into his hand. "Say Mama says hello. They're friends, you know."

This bit of information mattered to Billy. He nodded and gravely set out north for the Morris Location. When he found the Babić house, he didn't have to knock, because two younger boys hitting balls out front escorted him inside, one yelling, "Heh, Ma," and the other jumping around Billy like a hungry puppy.

Greeting him, Mrs. Babić mumbled niceties in broken English. She gave him a hunk of bread and nodded to him, her face a soft weary mix of peace and fret. Billy liked her face. She fixed the collar on his shirt for him and walked him to the door.

Tony was at work just then, so his mother set the letter on his bed and tried not to think about what it meant. Girls and boys in this country, it was something different to her. What had she known when she was a girl? She knew nothing. Or if she knew something, it was in her head and not in her experience. It was not notes to young men or going around together. She had never touched Jocco before they were married. And who would think where that would lead? As soon as she stopped nursing one baby, another one came along.

Marie didn't concern herself with what had happened when she was younger, who she used to be or who she might have been. What room was there for that kind of wandering? Marie Babić focused on what to do next and on getting it done. She heard the voices of her children around her like music and kept track of the weather and prayed for no trouble. Please dear God, she prayed, bring no trouble. Mary Mother of God, keep us from trouble.

She liked the Marković family. If Tony were to marry Vita Marković, that would make her happy. Maybe after they finished school and Tony got a job in the mine. They could live down the street at the Morris. Marie would like that, Tony down the street from her. And she would like being family with the Markovićs.

"Heh, Ma," Pete said, coming up close behind her. "What's the letter on Tony's bed? What kind of letter did that kid bring Tony?"

"You, shoo," she said. "Leave alone, Petey. Leave be."

And so Vita's note retained its mystery until Tony came home from work. His brothers hung around just to see what he would do with it, sure it was a love letter from Vita. But Tony read it with a worried face, then folded it with care before putting it into his shirt pocket. Two hours later, wearing a tie for the people of Bennet Park, he left to meet Vita.

"Why the secrecy" he asked, forgetting to tell her how pretty she looked. She always looked so good. More than he could believe half the time. "I can't come to the store anymore?"

"Not now."

Tony's stomach turned. Vita's father was undermining the best thing that had ever happened to him, this love with Vita, this glowing, perfectly smooth and unearthly person next to him. "What can I do?"

"He has his ideas, Tony. All we can do is stay out of his way. We can do that. We'll just meet around town and be together anyway." She held on to both of his hands. "Just like always, Tony."

He tried to act like always, but that was not the story unfolding here before him. Like always was the freedom to be together easily, Tony in and out of that warped screen door at the Marković store, seeing Vita's mom and siblings, taking in the smell of apples, sausage, and the rest, strolling Brooklyn or Park Addition or wherever they wanted without the darkness of her father's disapproval hovering like a midsummer storm. Meeting all over town? Hiding out? That was not for Tony Babić.

"Please don't make it too much, Tony. My father has his moods, but they come and go. Ma loves you." She snuggled into him, continuing to tug at him with steady eyes. "Don't worry."

So he pretended not to worry and gave himself to the moment, the sun low behind them and the trees so overpowering that he and Vita were mere shadows in their universe. Entangled, sweaty shadows that nobody in the park could see.

Tony returned to the Morris earlier than usual that night. Vita thought she should be home before nine and sent him on his trek along the Hull Rust when they were three blocks away from the store. His mother was rocking the baby when he came inside, and though she kept her pace, back and forth and back again, the floorboards creaking beneath her, she knew Tony was not happy. He took his heavy heart across the room and upstairs to his bed.

"G'night, Ma," he said, his voice weighing too much for a boy like Tony just out on a summer's night.

She watched him pass and continued to rock. He was her prize, this Tony, so smart and good and alive. Why would a boy like Tony come home sad? Where was the moon? his mother thought. Where was the moon pulling her Tony?

iii.

Tony awoke the next morning with a fierce determination. He would be with Vita no matter what her father thought of him or them. He wasn't going to mope—he was going to pursue. He would acquiesce to Vita's ideas, he decided, whatever it took to be together, and once that decision was made, he felt himself back on track. At work, he remained the same Tony Babić, the young man who could talk easily with customers and keep the counters clean, do anything they needed him to do. At home, he grabbed his younger brothers and swung them high, cradled his baby sister, hugged his mother, faced his father man to man.

"Pa, next summer I want to start working with you," he said, not in a childish pleading tone, but in a sure voice, a young man with a future's voice. Jocco never answered him either way. He gave him a glass of whiskey. Clapped him squarely on the back. This boy would make him proud, of that he was certain.

In this new elevation, Tony wrote to Luka. I'm doing good this summer, he said. My girlfriend loves me and I'm thinking of plans. How's Chicago? I'll come visit you again soon. He told

Luka that his sisters were well and growing up, that his mother had a new baby, that he liked his job and would be happy to finish school in a year and work for U.S. Steel. He didn't say he might want to be a cop. Luka's life seemed too far away now, too far to take Vita Marković, though she'd probably love that lake there. Don't get shot, Luka, he wrote at the end. Then as soon as he sealed the envelope he wished that he had not ended his letter that way. What kind of thing was that to say to a cop?

iv.

Whenever they could be together, Vita and Tony gravitated to their picnic table in the park. Far enough away from the pavilion on one side and Third Avenue on the other, and tucked beneath the pines, it seemed destined for them, placed there exactly for two people in love to be alone. Tony started bringing his jacket so they could spread it down beneath them, and Vita often wore a knit shawl to lay that down as well.

"Vita, it's August," her mother commented, seeing Vita wrapped in tightly stitched wool.

"It looks nice, Ma," she answered and that was true. It did, deep blue and fringed, and crisscrossed over Vita's lighter blue cotton dress.

"Seems too hot for a scarf," her mother added, but let it go. Mrs. Marković was grateful that Vita hadn't made any scenes after her father's ultimatum about Tony Babić. Of course Vita was still seeing the boy, but she was keeping the relationship away from the home, thank heaven. It was a good phrase—thank heaven. Mrs.

Marković had picked it up from one of her customers and now she used it every day. Thank heaven it had stopped raining or had finally started to rain, or the bewildered bear over on the tracks wandered elsewhere, or any number of mercies large and small which fell into the wondrous category of thank heaven.

"Where are you going tonight in your wool shawl then?"

Her daughter grinned. "Just to the park."

That last month before school started Tony and Vita did not go to the movies. They did not even stroll the park to hear the City Band. They nested behind the table, teased playfully on top of it, and one meeting at a time, lost themselves to each other. Without asking or discussing, they unbuttoned and undid, their bodies becoming more and more familiar and more unified. In their tangle of limbs and desire, Vita and Tony forgot who belonged to what or the fact that when they untangled, they would be two separate persons going two separate ways. It just didn't matter. They were young and lacking in experience and so did not calculate where this would go or what consequences they might face. Everything they did together felt right.

Tony repeated her name in gasps that caught in her hair and in her ear and in the still air around them. Vita found that when she and Tony were apart, she struggled to think of anything else. Nothing that occurred in her daily life, no action, encounter, or exchange, came close to the transformation of Tony's touch. That's what she thought. Her father's gorgeous ripening tomatoes, heavy on their stems, her mother's flowers in an array of pinks and purples, the often high, bright skies of August—these were nothing, nothing compared to the feeling she had. And the more intimate the two became, the more intimacy Vita wanted.

Her family noticed her preoccupation, but everyone had their own lives to consider, and Vita's dreaminess was not a priority. Her friend Kitty was another matter.

"I'm glad you have a boyfriend and all, Vita, but girlfriends are important too."

Vita had no answer. She was hanging clothes on the line and Kitty was following her as she did.

"Aren't you a little interested in what the rest of us mortals are doing?"

Vita breathed in the bleached clean of the pillowcases she was hanging. Poor Kitty and her earthly life. "How are you then?" she asked. That was all Kitty needed. She bounded off about the Italian boys and an argument she'd had with her mother over hem lengths and something regarding their friend Marguerite. Vita made an effort to listen, but she drifted toward Tony too often to know exactly what Kitty was saying.

"What about you" Kitty said at last. "What're you and Tony up to? Where do you even go that we never see you?"

Vita put her finger to her lips for Kitty to lower her voice. She tugged at her friend to move farther from the house. "My father told me I can't see Tony anymore. He says I'm too young and

Tony's from the locations, so that's why you don't see us. We try to avoid people."

Kitty was shocked. "And you didn't tell me this?"

"I just did, Kitty. We're trying not to be obvious."

Kitty popped the head of a clothespin in her mouth and sucked it like candy. "Sorry, Vita. Really. What does the Morris Location have to do with it?"

Vita shrugged. She didn't even want to say it out loud, this superior attitude her father had about the mining locations and those that lived there. That they were rough. Houses were flimsy. It would all come apart in a chance gust of wind. She looked past the washing she'd hung and past the flat back of the store.

"I love Tony," Vita said quietly. "It's incredible how I feel. I had no idea I could feel this way."

It wasn't until Vita had finished her task and the two sat down together on the grass at the edge of the yard that Kitty gave her warning. "Be careful how far you go, Vita."

"How far?"

"You know, physically." Kitty ducked her head low and whispered, "You don't want to get pregnant. What would your dad do then?"

Vita held her breath. She didn't understand what Kitty meant exactly, but she didn't want her friend to think she was stupid about boys, when here she was, near naked with Tony almost every night. "I'm not going to get pregnant," she answered. "We're not even married."

Kitty whacked her thigh. "Good God, what does that have to do with it? You go all the way and you can get pregnant whether you're married or not. Or if you even know the guy. It's biology, Vita. You took biology."

"I did." Vita concentrated on the clothes flapping slightly in the afternoon breeze, the sleeves on the shirts seeming to have a life of their own.

"How do you know so much, Kitty?"

"I just do. I listen all the time. You know me. My cousin Lucille got pregnant and had to get married. It was a big deal. You hear these stories too, Vita. She had to rush to get married and make it right. You need to pay more attention to the world."

"Yes," Vita said in return, but she wondered if it was too late for that already.

Hours later she held tightly to Tony again, unable to think about what was right or not right and without any wish to stop their forward tumble.

v.

Once it happened, as soon as it happened, Vita knew. She knew they'd gone, as Kitty had warned, too far. They'd gone too far. There was a moment, though later she couldn't exactly find that moment, when their closeness, the lost pleasures and wet skin had all become a painful, shocking, and otherworldly sort of connection. The perfect night sky, her eyes opening to that blanket of stars she'd known all her life, and the last wobbling notes of the City Band way, way across the park. Tony repeating her name. "Vita," he said, "I love you."

And she loved him. That she knew too. They'd crossed a divide together, whatever it was, and they loved each other even more than before. Or they would certainly love each other more because of this.

Neither of them moved. Her arms locked around him and her legs curved in and out of his legs and there they stayed. The ground got colder and the music stopped. They heard voices, but none of them nearby. And after a bit they heard nothing at all other than their own small rustlings to be comfortable, to adjust against the hard ground and the cooling air. Tony slept for a few minutes, exhausted by their feverish time.

"Tony," Vita whispered, "I need to go home."

"I wish we could stay here forever."

"Maybe if we were on a bed," she said laughing. Her body hurt from lying on the ground and between her legs from where Tony had been.

"One more year of school and then we can get married."

"Seems like a long time away." She was pulling on her clothing. "We have a whole winter to get through and nowhere to go."

"I'll find a place. I'll figure it out." He had no idea where he would find a place for the two of them to come together in the middle of the winter. Or the chill of fall even. In his world, as in Vita's, there were no extra rooms, no empty spaces waiting for them in the dark. He had no idea. Still he believed in his own ingenuity. "I'll find us something," he said again.

"It's late, Tony." Vita walked faster ahead of him out of the park, and he kept pace, holding her hand and dreaming about when he would see her next.

"Don't worry," he said. He went with her to the corner of her block and watched her go through the back door of the store. Then he waited. There were no loud voices from within, no explosions of disapproval, and after a while, the two lights that had been on upstairs were turned off, leaving the house dark.

When Tony turned to head home, he saw a distant figure coming his way, a cigarette making one tiny red flare in the shadows of the boulevard trees. Tony stepped into a neighboring yard to watch George Marković pass by.

It had been the most miraculous night of his life, even more so than looking out at Chicago's lake with Luka. Love was miraculous.

He'd never be the same again.

ORDER

My father-in-law made his money on property. He knew how to take a risk and make it play for him. Then he'd go visit his friends at the bank, dried paint on his shoes, undershirt half-buttoned. He'd sit across from the bank president and talk about money. Talk about where things were going, how to shuffle the deck. What the hell do I know? I never owned a house in my life until my in-laws left us theirs. Never wanted the debt. Never cared for the risk. But the old man was a different story.

His wife would try and stop him from going downtown looking like a bum. He had good shirts, ties, a nice suit. "We all shita the same," he'd say and back his shining Packard out of the garage so slow you'd think he was driving solid gold. Off he'd go, hat hardly sticking up above the steering wheel.

I didn't start out thinking we're all the same. I started out thinking there was a top and a bottom. Italians like my father-in-law weren't at the top. But if they made money and spoke plain English, even a little plain English, then maybe. My old man wasn't at the top. But he was a supervisor and a pioneer. He was one of the first to come to town, so he had some respect. The top tended to be the Scandinavians. Not so much Finlanders, but Swedes and the others. We had our names for each other back then. Now nobody cares. Now we start worrying about the next bunch coming in from somewhere else. Now they're at the bottom.

We all lived on this same small dot of the map. Maybe if you were from Minneapolis or Chicago, you thought everyone on our small dot was connected—tough climate and hard work, near isolation up north here. My son drives more miles to get to his golf course than half the people here do in a month or a year or ever. Who had a way to go anywhere back then or even anywhere they wanted to go? Maybe locations like Morris were never far from the center of town and were pretty much part of the town at large, but they were off on their own too. People who lived there went there and most everyone else did not. My wife never went to a mining location all the years she was growing up. Her friends lived across the street right in the middle of town, maybe two streets down. Not on the far sides of the Hull Rust. Those of us on the locations, we were a different breed. We felt proud of that. Maybe others saw different.

The family story was that Vita Marković's old man thought he was a little further toward the top than we were. He had a store in town, sometimes played cards with Swedes and Norwegians. Maybe he thought that anyone living on a location was down a notch from anyone living in the center of town, though their block in Brooklyn was never what I'd call the center of anyplace. But that's how people were. I guess that's how they always are. Someone's up and someone's down. Call it order.

The Markovićs were Croatian just like us, went to the same church, belonged to the same Croatian Union here in town. But George Marković didn't like his daughter dating Tony. That's the story. The prize of our family wasn't good enough for his family living three to a room on top of a grocery store. How do you argue with that? If it was even true. What if old man Marković just didn't want his pretty daughter Vita dating anyone? What if it's not a story about who's up and who's down, but only a story of men guarding their daughters?

I did think my wife's family was better than my own back when I met them. I might have told her that. But she had a dad who didn't see those differences and neither did she. She was always good to my family, reached out. And some of them loved her, that's the truth. My dad lit up when she came to see them. They had a little house in town by then and my wife would stop with cake or bars, the stuff she was always baking. My mother loved sweets. She was tired out by then, Ma was, by the time I got married and my wife brought sweets. All those kids and the boarders, everything that happened with Tony, and then all her boys but Pete off to war, three sons in the war at the same time. My two brothers ran into each other at the Battle of the Bulge, if you can believe it. Georgie looked out across the road and there was Nikko marching along. Or that's how that story goes. One came back a soldier for life, kept his uniform, bought vintage war Jeeps, drove them around in parades. The other came back and said nothing.

But we all came back. And after all she lived through, my mother seemed happy to roam her little house and eat the sweets my wife brought over. When I'd talk to her, she'd barely know what I was saying. "Johnny," she'd mutter and nod and nod some more in that way people do when they have nothing to say.

Markovićs, I've known them all my life. Big families in small towns, they disperse, let me tell you, and everywhere you look there's someone from this family or that. Kids of kids. Now grandkids, I suppose, and kids of grandkids. The names stick. I can run into a Marković at Super One or the golf course, at Checco's Bar, church, or the Howard Café. Everyone's fine, everyone's friends. We been here forever now and we're all part of the order.

But in 1928, maybe not. I can't say. I was just a kid tossing balls in the street and waiting to grow up and be just like my big brother. That's what I was thinking then. I wanted to be just like Tony.

FOUR

Fall 1928 to Early 1929

i.

Maybe Al Capone didn't care about the Black underground on the South Side, but he watched his Irish rivals on the North Side closely. On the morning of Valentine's Day 1929, his key Irish competitor, Bugs Moran by name, hurried in the cold to a warehouse at Clark and Division to check on one of his bootlegging operations. Minutes before he arrived, the seven men waiting for him there—his brother-in-law, the owner of the warehouse, an optometrist who enjoyed the dangers of gang affiliations, and four others—all were shoved against the concrete wall and shot in the back. The men who fired on them wore police uniforms, though of course, they were not the police. Bugs Moran escaped, but it shook the core of his operation and marked the beginning of his downfall.

"Had to be Capone," went the buzz around the city the minute the news hit the streets, though Al Capone claimed he'd been at the dog track in Florida when it happened.

"As long as they kill off each other and leave the rest of us alone," the cops in Luka's district repeated all day.

"John May went to school with me," Danny Cox told him when they heard the names of the men who were shot. "He's got all these kids, Luka. Six, maybe seven kids."

"So was he part of Moran's gang?"

Danny shook his head as if Johnny May had been his own brother. "Suppose he was, Luka, Jesus. Johnny May."

Luka and Danny were wrapping up their shift with the last of the day's coffee pot. "I'll tell you what I think, Luka. No way Johnny was a hardened killer like some of those guys. You can't make me believe it."

"People change though, Danny. Money, pressures, who knows."

"I don't believe it," Danny said again, continuing to shake his head in denial.

"You think they picked today because of Saint Valentine?" Luka had been wondering about this since he heard the news. Was there a message they were supposed to understand, some angle the cops and public at large were missing here?

"What the hell does that have to do with it, Luka? If these guys even know what day is what anyhow."

"Valentine was a martyr, Danny. That's the story."

"Yeah. Well, there's always a story." Danny fastened his coat and went home.

It had been a cloudy day, cold and gray and full of bad news.

But Luka had a date with Kata that night. They'd had dinner together on New Year's Eve and she'd been so thrilled. She'd never been to a New Year's Eve celebration of any kind, she'd told him. So he'd asked her to dinner again. She seemed even more pleased about going out with him on Valentine's Day.

He didn't have a romantic feeling for Kata, though he wasn't sure why. She was attractive and feminine. He loved her modern sense of style, her couple of decorated hats, and the way she turned her coat collar up in a dashing sort of manner. She was always polite, kind even, smiled often and easily. She appeared to like him, seemed happy to see him and interested in his opinions. He did not understand his hesitancy. He had wondered how his friend Danny had felt about his wife before they were married but had never asked.

He picked Kata up at her rooming house, and they walked many blocks to a small Polish restaurant that had caught his eye when he'd passed it on the job. The walls inside were rough stone, the tables covered in cloths. For Valentine's Day, the owners had lit candles and hired an accordion player who stood in the back playing lyrical tunes that Luka did not recognize. Kata wore her New Year's Eve dress again, and this time he noticed how it draped on her shoulders against the creaminess of her skin.

"That's really a nice dress, Kata," he told her as they sat at a small table facing one another.

"I saw it in the window at Marshall Field's and made it myself. I like sewing clothes." She adjusted her posture to lengthen her neck. "I'm good at it too." She smiled sweetly, as he knew her to do. "I could make you a shirt sometime, Luka. It would be different for me, but I know I could do it."

"That's very generous," he answered, and they pattered on from there the way they always did, making simple conversation with little meaning, but significant comfort. His cop friends weren't interested in what he ate for breakfast or how often he did his laundry or what his mother had to say in her last letter. But those things were the stuff of Kata's life, the essence of daily survival and grounding. They spent at least ten full minutes discussing the menu items, what looked good to them, what foods they knew and didn't know, and how similar many of the items on the menu were to the Croatian food their families made back home.

Occasionally when they were together Kata would ask how was work, but something told him she didn't want more than the most simple answer. Kata was not a woman who fed on drama. She might know of the gang killings and Chicago's powerful underground, but he doubted she would want to think about it let alone discuss it with him over dinner. Kata liked good news. Or maybe no news. And so Luka left his work and worries back in his room along with his badge and his gun.

They talked and ate until Kata said she'd need to be up early in the morning for work. He watched her pull on her gloves, adjusting them finger by finger until they fit perfectly. They left the restaurant side by side, but Luka did not reach out for her hand as he thought he might—or should. At her door, he kissed her lightly and made his way back to his apartment alone. He liked walking with a purpose, moving toward a destination, even if it was his own cramped room with a banging radiator.

The next day Police Commissioner Russell and Attorney General Swanson began their search for evidence on the Valentine's Day Massacre. On the streets, rumors ran wild. Some said Moran's Irish gang had been amassing more power after killing Capone's ally Tony Lombardo back in September. That was one theory. Some said Moran was going after Capone's liquor sources in Detroit. That was another theory. The men waiting at the warehouse had apparently thought the "cops" were coming by to negotiate, with no suspicion that they were there to gun them down.

Accustomed to violence, the city of Chicago nonetheless reacted to the Valentine's Day Massacre more than they had to other gang killings over the preceding decade. These men were all gangsters, sure, but the cop disguises, the midmorning ambush, the blatant execution-style killings—this was another low, even for Chicago. Everyone in the criminal justice system summoned a renewed energy to stop gang warfare and, in particular, the rampant power of Alphonse Capone.

 Luka felt this too. He was tired of pretending he fit in with his friends on the take. He'd been in America for almost seven years. Many days he forgot he was Croatian, forgot the five thousand miles he'd traveled and the verbs and history he'd had to learn. He was an American cop. Like he'd dreamed. But when he left

Brusane, he took with him the ancient seriousness of the old country. His mother could hardly wait to raise her Jesus from the dead every Easter and pray through the long months for Him to be born again on Christmas Eve. That was enough for her. Dear Jesus was enough. Her life that uncomplicated, that clean. He tried to think if his life had felt that way back then too. Even if it wasn't, he was here now. A cop who wanted to fight crime as he'd told everyone he'd known for all these years.

In the wake of the Saint Valentine's Day Massacre, the Chicago Police Department formed a crime lab, the first in the country, funded by a sixty-thousand-dollar grant and run in partnership with the law department at Northwestern University. The cops buzzed about it. Solving crime under a microscope? Clothing fibers and skin particles? Danny Cox rolled his Irish blue eyes. But to the high-stakes detectives working for the city and the nation's Bureau of Investigation, this crime lab was a godsend, allowing them to examine the most minute details of grisly crimes. It made Chicago a leader in pursuing violent crimes. And it gave Luka an idea for his future.

He wrote to the Bureau of Investigation in Washington, DC, requesting an application to become a federal agent. He was certain they wanted exemplary cops just like him. Cops who made their regulation pay and stayed on the right side of the rules. In turn, Luka wanted to work for the organization that was at the forefront of criminal apprehension in the country. He told no one, not even Kata. Like the money he'd hidden under his mattress at Marie Babić's boardinghouse, this was his secret.

ii.

In September, Tony quit the football team. The meat market asked him to work more hours for the fall butchering and that suited his plans more than running around the field and rolling in dirt—or being relegated to the bench to watch the team's heroes win or lose. Nobody in his family noticed or cared other than his kid brothers who plain liked the idea of having a big brother on the high school football team. Jocco had never been to any game Tony played, maybe because he didn't really know football. And if he did, it certainly was nothing in his world.

Tony was beginning to have an idea that it wasn't part of his world either, no matter that he was strong and fast. He didn't quite have the moves. His hand-me-down shoes were always formed to fit someone else's foot and he wasn't driven to ram and tackle. He wasn't a star.

"I liked seeing you at the games, though," Vita said with an unmistakable flash of disappointment.

"I can make more money now, Vita."

Money was a real topic. Everyone in their mining town strove to make money and more money, take on extra work, stay longer hours, push for higher wages. From the president of the bank to the newest guy on Jocco's track gang, money was a guiding light in life, the object of desire and a pulsing beacon just there ahead. They'd crossed an ocean and half the country to be where they were and all because they believed they'd make money.

"America," an old woman remarked to Vita one day in the store, "there's gold in the streets in America. You hear me girl?" Vita had nodded without thinking. "You see any gold here?" the woman went on, sweeping her arm in a broad half circle to all corners of the Marković store. "You see?"

Vita answered that she did not. "What I mean," the woman said and poked her index finger into the air, "you want gold? You got to get the gold." Then as the woman left the store, Vita heard her mutter, "Crazy men."

That gray afternoon, Vita had watched the lady, bundled in a thick cloth coat and red fringed head scarf, as she made her way between the snowbanks and out to the road. Probably talking to herself all the way, Vita thought. Now here was Tony saying the same thing. "You want gold in the streets?" she asked him.

He thought she was making a joke. "Sure, Vita. And on these sidewalks too."

She didn't laugh.

She went to the season's first football game to watch boys who were not her love and tried to make conversation with Kitty and Marguerite as though she felt as carefree as they seemed to feel and her life was as uncomplicated as theirs. It was late summer, early fall, a time when the leaves turned and the air cooled and another season stirred. The crowd around Vita jumped up every few minutes to yell at the players, their own or the visiting team, she couldn't tell which. Cheers continued to rock the bleachers. It was a new school year and everyone loved a good roar into the night.

Vita no longer fit the scene. She no longer had a boyfriend in the game, if only sitting on a bench below the crowd. Tony was off helping cut up a cow or hog on a farm she didn't know, preparing meat for a store that competed with her own family's store, and making money more important to him than she could understand.

"You're a dreamer," her older sister had always said to her. "You're a dreamer, Vita." She was the one in her family prone to the illusory, she knew this, staring off out windows, following patterns of light, even the swirl of dust floating around in the store. Now this dreaminess of hers leaned toward Tony and the gauzy cocoon they had spun for themselves. But where it would lead was another matter. Kitty had warned her. Her father had warned her, in his own way. Tony reassured her. Here at the game, the fans jumped up every time their home team made a tackle or run as if it were all life and death. Yet it was only a game. And everyone knew it.

She didn't think this bond with Tony was a game, a win-or-lose game. They had no rules and no cheering fans, no lights with numbers flashing the score. "Vita," Kitty yelled in her ear, "did you see that? Did you see that touchdown? Oh, my gosh." She beamed as if it were her own doing. "Quit dreaming and watch the game, Vita." Kitty was up on her feet cheering again. "You're such a dreamer." Vita stayed seated on the wooden bleacher and shrugged. She guessed she was a dreamer. Her dream was to be with Tony, but no matter how she concentrated on that dream, she could not give it a shape. Falling in love had been something she could define, a dream come true. Now here they were, without a place or a purpose or even a date to the Friday night football game.

Tony's dream, however, was beginning to take a very clear shape. He wanted to be a man. He was tired of being Jocco's son, tired of being sidelined in football and quietly acquiescent in school. Tired of following orders that led him to nowhere and nothing and being a star only to that bunch of ruffians out at the Morris. He was ready to be a man. And he was determined.

Coming home after his long day, he found Jocco sitting on the stoop, puffing a cigar. Tony stopped to sit with him. "I hate killing chickens," he said, taking a breath of the smoke circling him. "You ever kill a chicken, Pa?"

Jocco laughed without cheer, his gums exposed as they were when he laughed. "Woman's work," he proclaimed and slapped Tony's back and laughed again. "They pay you for that?"

"Not much. They mean well though." Tony glanced sideways to

see if he should risk his question. "Why don't you get me a job at the mine, Pa. That's good money. Real money. No draining blood out of dead chickens in the mines."

"Ha, Tony. You think it's all money? You ready for that kind of work? Ready for night shifts? Ready to quit school where you got all those words of yours? The universe, you say. Discipline, you say. I hear you." Jocco chuckled at his own wit. "Half the guys in the mine don't speak English, you know. They could give a shit for the universe, Tony."

"I know enough words now, Pa. I know math and what the world looks like, geography and that. I can find things on the map."

"The world don't look like this, I'll tell you that." His old man scanned the dirt road that ran down the center of the Morris and sucked his cigar. "The world don't look like the Hull Rust. Maybe nothing does."

"That's what I mean, Pa. We've got history here too. I don't have to have a book for history."

Jocco really laughed at that one. "What kind of history, Tony? By god you got ideas."

Tony didn't have an answer. His father was a smart man and wily as a fox. He'd been born in one country, crossed an ocean with whatever ideas of his own he'd never shared, and had lived in Ontario, Canada, and here in Minnesota. And he wasn't dead yet. He wasn't done making the history of Jocco Babić, that was for sure. That's what Tony knew. The ore pit was like no other.

He had learned that in school. And the ore they mined traveled far, he had learned that too.

Jocco held the butt of the cigar high above his head. "My boy, the dreamer."

He stood, pitched his cigar, and went inside.

That September 1928, the Oliver Mining Company was booming and the town was booming and all the local businesses as well. Tony's request for work was not unreasonable. Jocco considered this. Maybe there were young men who went off to be educated and came back to run things around town, but not the boys Jocco knew. Not the boys at the Morris or Carson locations, Leetonia, Pool, or Penobscot either. If you learned work, then that is what you did. Tony wanted to work and be a man. Well, so why not?

Jocco mulled this for days, and finally decided to see what he could do. He caught a ride on a truck to talk to one of the other foremen about a spot for Tony, to find out what was possible. "He's smart, my Tony," Jocco said with confidence. "And strong. Like bull," he added and laughed out loud. Then he stayed for a while, discussing the politics of the mine, where the Oliver was putting extra men, who was squawking at who these days, all of that.

"We'll see," Jocco's co-worker repeated at every pause, his face covered with ore dust, snuff tucked in the corner of his jaw. "We'll see, Jocco."

Jocco worked late that night. He came home, washed up, and sat alone with Marie at the long table to eat what she put before him. "Tony wants to work," he said to her in Croatian, what they did to keep their conversations between themselves. "Wants to be a man now."

Across from him, Marie's eyes were on the aching joints of her hands which she rubbed the whole while. "He's a boy, Tony." She wanted to say "my boy," but she did not. Her first one who lived, she wanted to add, but she did not say that either.

"He's seventeen now. You think he's a boy forever?" Jocco continued with his cabbage soup.

"He has school, books." She stared at her hands, her nails clipped to the finger and white as a bleached sheet. "You think Tony leaves his school?"

"He wants to work."

"He works," Marie argued, a woman who never thought to argue with anyone. But for Tony, she wanted to argue. "He works pretty good," she said again.

"Chickens and pigs! That's no work for Tony, stara." He called her old woman as he sometimes did, an endearment in his mind.

"No," she answered, giving her head a sharp shake of disapproval. "My Tony. He stays with school. Stays with the books."

Jocco shut up. Marie would lose this battle. Tony had already moved past his boyhood. He had some girl, he had his geography, here and there, his letters to a cop in Chicago. Who would stop a boy like that from getting a real job and going to work every day with real men? "Good soup," he said to Marie, a rare compliment to show his sympathy. She'd lost all those babies to get to Tony and now he would move on to a life without her. "You come to bed?" he asked. Her losses made him want what she had for him under that worn dress of hers.

She cleared his dishes, mumbled prayers he could not hear and followed her husband.

But she did not leave the topic of Tony. She took it with her into the bed and held onto it as she put her tired arms around Jocco and went with him the way he liked to go. She could never say no to Jocco. He didn't care if her mind roamed elsewhere. To her Tony with an open book, making his lists, learning things she'd never know, his head bobbing in thought, her Tony. He would end this now?

Jocco rolled away, deep in sleep, his snores as loud and regular as his breathing. He was not a quiet man even when he slept. Jocco was big, imposing, alive with himself and his world of work and men. Men boarders and men neighbors and his men friends and now Tony too. That's what Jocco said. Tony wanted to be a man.

So maybe she would have a son who was a man. Maybe he would marry the Marković girl and live nearby, down the block at the Morris, and stop by for a slice of her bread out of the oven. She went around and around like a spinning wheel. It was this, it could be that. Or that, then this. She'd lose or not.

She'd left the window cracked open for fresh air like they did in Brusane. To keep the sickness away. In between Jocco's snores, she listened for the baby's breath, sleeping in her bed in the corner of the room. Such a good baby. Tony would be a man and Marie would still have this little girl to raise up. She might like books too. Who was to know? What came next and next after that, Marie lay awake wondering.

At the Marković house, Vita's mother did not worry about her daughter and Tony Babić. She was certain the relationship continued, though Vita was leaving no trail. Mrs. Marković considered Vita the most obvious of all her children, the least covert. She had been easily obedient, unlike her sisters who tended to grab on to a bit of contention whenever they could. Her son, Billy, while not contentious, had notions in his head all the time, thinking, thinking big thoughts his mother was sure. Vita was her child who said yes to her mother and smiled always at customers and seemed pleased with her lot and herself and her dreamy dreams, gazing out windows and singing songs.

So Mrs. Marković did not probe. When Vita left the store alone, saying, "I'll be back soon," her mother waved and let it be. When Vita returned at any reasonable hour, Mrs. Marković mumbled a thank heaven and nothing more. And oddly, or perhaps not so oddly, her husband never asked if Vita was still seeing the Babić boy. He had stated his rule. It seemed not to occur to him that he would be so wholly ignored.

iii.

Temperatures took a turn early as they often did in the North. Almost overnight the ground hardened and birds quieted in the trees. Bennet Park was no longer an option for Tony and Vita to be hidden and alone, and although they'd known this would happen, had both dreaded this change, each had conjured a different solution.

"Kitty told me nobody uses that shed out back of her house now that the garden is down for the winter." This was Vita's solution. "We could fix that up for ourselves. She says her family doesn't even pay attention to it all winter."

They sat side by side on a second-floor staircase at school, in the wing reserved for junior college classes. Nobody knew them there. Nobody cared that they were there or what they were discussing.

"Love with shovels and rakes," Tony responded, not at all excited about the possibility of coming together in a garden shed. She clearly was. In her mind, she'd already claimed that shed, swept away cobwebs, spiders and dirt, then laid flat one of her mother's rag rugs—and maybe folded a couple of moth-eaten blankets on top of the rug. It occurred to Tony that she may be thinking of hanging a curtain over a window, if she happened to have one.

Tony was aiming higher. He wanted to settle them in a house living a real life together, not sneaking into Kitty's garden shed. "Tony?" She slid down one step, the better to see him. "What are you thinking?"

He didn't know what to say. Was he going to ask her to marry him sitting on a school stairway with a stack of books on his lap? "I was thinking something better for us," he said finally, turning to face her and hoping not to fall into her eyes and get lost there as so often happened to him with Vita. He breathed in and pulled his shoulders back, then reached for her hand. "Maybe it's time to be together for real."

She did not register what he was saying.

"In a house," he added.

Vita jerked away from him. "We can't buy a house, Tony. I don't understand."

He lowered his voice. "I want to work for Oliver Mining. Then I'll have money to get a house. We could rent a house. Or if I work at the mine, I might get a location house. Maybe we could live at the Morris."

"Now?" She shook her head not knowing she was doing this.

"In our last year of school, Tony? When we're so close to graduating?"

Her reaction riled him. "Vita, what's the difference if we finish school? We already know more than anyone in our families and half the people in town. Think of everything we know." He smacked the stack of books on his lap, the books he had cherished for years that suddenly meant so little. "What more do we need?"

Her voice dropped to a hiss. "What if I want a diploma, Tony? My sister quit and now what? She works in the grocery and sews clothes and doesn't even have a place to wear them. What does she have? I want a diploma. I want to be the one who graduates and show my little sisters and Billy that this is what you do. This is America. We're not some old country poor people who have to go to work to support the family. Your dad is a foreman. My dad has the grocery and I know I have to help out and I always do, but I want to finish school and say I have a diploma. Even if all I do is nail it to the wall."

This made Tony furious. "What's more important, Vita, a diploma that gets you nothing or starting a life, a real life together?" He struggled to keep his temper in check. "You think you'll go to college here?" With his arm, he cut the air in front of them. Two college boys in shirts and ties passed them conversing intensely and laughing easily. "That's what people do with diplomas, Vita. They go get more diplomas, you know that? And those diplomas cost money and who even knows what guys like them will do with those diplomas?" He stopped talking only to get his breath. Vita sat frozen, glaring and unhappy.

"You're saying we quit school right now and get married. And you work for the Oliver, which you don't even have a job yet, and then what do I do out of school with no diploma? Go live in some house at the Morris and wait for you to come around after the graveyard shift—or some double shift? I hear people talk, Tony. I know how those mining jobs go with guys working night and day. If you want to quit school and get a job at the Oliver Mine, then you go do that." She stood up and adjusted her skirt. "While you're doing that, I will finish school and help out in the grocery and tell Kitty that maybe some other couple truly in love can make use of the shed out back of her house."

Tony grabbed Vita's hand and pulled her back onto the step. "Shhh," he whispered. "Please don't get excited. Don't get mad, Vita. I thought it was a good thing, me and you in a house. You want to turn Kitty's shed into a house? Add on a kitchen or something." He gave her his most playful grin. "Would that work?" He ran his hand up and down along her arm so gently. "Vita?"

"Oh pooh, Tony!" She whacked him lightly in return. "Of course I want to be with you," she said and, without warning, started to cry. "It was such a summer, wasn't it? I want things to be like that. I want to be with you all the time. I can barely think straight lately. But I thought I would be the one to finish, Tony. And you too. What it would mean to your ma—and mine." Her eyes held him, so serious and certain.

This time, he was the one to pull back. He didn't want to think about disappointing his mother or setting a bad example for his younger brothers. But work in the mines was real. He needed to be a man with a real life now. Looking down to the books on his lap, he said, "Napoleon conquered Italy. Isn't that a thing to know? Something to talk about to the Italians around town." He smiled at her, but his shoulders had sunk into a curve of defeat. "Long live Napoleon."

That was the end of the conversation. Neither of them forgot it, however. It was consequential. Not just some bump in their relationship, but a division. And they both recognized this division, all the while pretending they did not.

The next Saturday night after he was done working at the meat market, Tony met Vita in the shed behind Kitty's. She had a bundle of blankets that she had managed to smuggle out of the house and carry down the block to Kitty's. The sun had already set and the night sky's stars scattered far and high above them, though inside the shed they missed this spectacle. Vita had, in fact, come by earlier to clean it up and was ready now for them to make this rickety wooden building something their own. Tony had missed her body so, he seized on the strange, cold privacy and her smooth skin and escaped into the moment.

Vita wrapped herself around him, imagining they were travelers on a wide plain, stopped for the night in this shack along the way, all the world on the other side of the frosted walls and all of life, their future and its impossibilities held close beneath her mother's threadbare blankets.

Every few days afterward, Tony sought out Jocco and asked, "What do you know about a job for me, Pa? Anything new?"

Sometimes his mother heard him ask his father about a job in the mine. Her son's words would catch her in the midst of her work, inciting her to launch into immediate prayers to the Blessed Mother, her Hail Mary, Mother of Gods loud and clear in Croatian, which the rest of the family could translate or not as they pleased.

iv.

George Marković kept his store open long hours as the holidays approached. He stocked his wife's preserves and baked goods, he cured the meats he knew his regulars loved, and put signs in the front window announcing daily specials. He recognized, as did merchants at all levels in town, that come January his sales would drop as mining families hunkered down for the worst two months of the year. He set a schedule for his kids to work long shifts from six every morning through ten every night.

For that reason, Vita found herself behind the counter with one of her younger sisters most evenings. The shed over at Kitty's now had a thin layer of frost at every gap in its construction. Her footprints and Tony's lay deep and obvious leading up and away from the door. Kitty said she'd told her ma she was storing Christmas surprises there, which accounted for the scatter of steps in the snow.

"Did she believe you?" Vita asked.

Kitty leaned over the counter at Marković Grocery. "Oh, sure.

She's too busy not to believe me and anyway," Kitty went on, "I don't think she'd care if she found out it was you and Tony."

"I care though."

"There's no shame in love, Vita. I wish it were me. What do you think of this scarf I knit?"

Kitty was wrapped in such an audacious mix of colors that Vita had not wanted to mention it. "Nice tight stitches," she offered.

"No, not nice stiches, Vita. Beautiful colors. Don't you think really? I took all the leftovers from Ma's knitting basket and put them together. Italians love color, you know."

Vita doubted those Italian boys that Kitty wanted to impress could be won over by a mix of gaudy colors on a scarf, but who was she to say. Personally she thought Kitty looked like she belonged on the clown float in the Fourth of July parade. Still, watching her friend twirl the fringed ends of her bizarre creation, Vita envied Kitty's hope for love, her anticipation of its first thrill, the possibilities she imagined while not ever having to contend with its reality.

"You going to a Christmas party?" Vita asked.

Kitty sighed with great drama. "Maybe."

Vita wished for a maybe. She knew for a fact that she would not be going to any parties and, outside of occasional liaisons at school, she would not be seeing Tony any time soon either. Yet when the store was empty of customers, how she could dally in thoughts of love. She'd drift off to the fact of Tony's heat, his hands hot even in the cold of that uncomfortable garden shed, his mouth finding her, his fingers entwined with hers and the way she'd shiver in want. At those times in the quiet store, Vita's gaze would float over the fruit crates stacked sideways, on the shelves her father had built and on all the jars of pickles, beets, beans, and corn, on brushes for cleaning and wrapped bars of strong soap, seeing none of it. She always saw herself with Tony. That's all she saw.

Years before her father had pounded a strap on the door with horse bells attached. That way, when customers entered, the family would know it, even if they were upstairs, out back, or bent over boxes of unpacked stock. Now the bell continually yanked Vita out of her visions and back to matters at hand. Back to groceries and neighbors needing this or that and the cash register pinging open and shut as she tucked in the money.

One week before Christmas, Jocco got word of a job for Tony and sent his son to the Oliver Mining office to apply. "It's labor, Tony," he said, his eyes sizing up his son. "You think you know hard work?" Maybe Jocco thought his oldest son was too soft, too much his mother's boy with all her Hail Marys and worry. But Tony only laughed deep and large. Hard work, even lousy, dirty, backbreaking work, was still work. Every man in the mines at least knew that.

The foreman who interviewed him was a stranger, not a Croat, not a friend of Jocco's and not from the Morris. He felt familiar to Tony anyway. He loomed taller and wider than his actual height and width the way Jocco always did. He scanned Tony in that same humorless way. This man had lost a few teeth, the tip of a finger, half his hair, and, Tony was to find out later, half of his children to illness and accident. "You do whatever we need you to do," he said. "It's shoveling rock, it's filling holes with mud, it's whatever we need you to do. Keep your eyes open. Things move here. They move fast."

He had locked on to Tony the entire time he spoke. "Things move here, Babić."

Tony nodded and continued to nod. Things moved. They moved fast. Anything he said might come out wrong, too loud or not loud enough or impertinent—another word he learned in school that he would now set aside—or unsure or too cocky. These men like Jocco and the foreman had seen everything and lived everything and kids like Tony reminded them how far they'd traveled and how little the young understood.

"Start day after Christmas. Night shift." He gave Tony the specific time and place and what to bring with him and then escorted him out into the light of day where it had started to snow. They did not shake hands. The foreman spit a wad of snuff and walked back to work.

"No good, Tony," his mother responded to his news. She said this in clear English, to make sure he understood what she said. "No good," she repeated in the same way she said prayers, that near chant to herself, to God and his only begotten son Jesus.

She kept her eyes on her work, her hands busy, as joy like water squeezed out and away from her. Jocco was right to call her old woman. Poor old woman she already was and now this.

Vita's response was worse.

He waited until they were underneath their coats and the blankets in Kitty's garden shack, waited for the sublimity of their bodies together before he muttered the words into her wayward curls, as though speaking an endearment or more, beckoning her further into his world and their world. "Vita," he said, "I have a job at the mine now." Strands of her hair caught in his mouth as he spoke and for a short second, maybe less—though it seemed long enough to encourage him—she did not speak or tighten or pull herself away. But then she did.

"You didn't tell me."

"I am telling you, Vita. I'm telling you now. It just happened."

The only light in the shack came from stars visible through the one window and in that slice of heavenly light, Tony saw Vita's anger as she sat upright, pulling her clothing together and herself, smashing a hat onto her hair, saying nothing more to him. She stood, folding the blankets decisively until she and all her possessions were done with him.

"It did not just happen, Tony. You wanted this and you went after it and now all I can say is good for you." She opened the creaky door. "And Merry Christmas."

He sat against the ice wall of the shed, stunned, half-dressed and unsure of himself. Had he just lost Vita? Did love end that simply, the wrong words, an angry response, a door flung open and closed—the moment over? He dressed as though he'd never dressed before, fumbling with his buttons, not wanting to let go of this awful place where at least he'd loved Vita time and again those past two months.

Leaving, he fastened the door lock and trudged down the block to Markovič's Grocery, where the store lights remained on and, from a certain angle, he could see George Markovič sweeping the floor and Mrs. Markovič at the counter talking to a woman that so reminded Tony of his mother, he had to stop himself from thinking it so.

He returned to the Morris not sad so much as numb. Of course Vita had objected to his idea of getting a job at the mine that fall. But then they'd let the topic go and, in his own mind, he'd come around to believing she would accept his idea in time. They would continue to meet. They would come together on the floor of the garden shed. And he would continue to feel her love surprising and deep and true.

The next day he quit school and on Wednesday, December 26, 1928, he reported to work as a laborer for Oliver Mining.

v.

On Valentine's Day, Vita's English teacher read the class poems. They were all about love, mostly incomprehensible and otherwise heartbreaking. *If all the world and love were young, And truth in every shepherd's tongue, These pretty pleasures* and on and on, he read. *To live with thee and be thy love.* Vita chewed on her pencil, unconsciously ate her eraser. *How do I love thee? Let me count the ways.*

The English teacher, Mr. Dryer, wore wire-rimmed glasses and spoke with exaggerated diction, a man who would have liked a stage for recitation and an audience more apprehending than a room of high school students whose parents mostly mined for ore. Mr. Dryer relished every syllable of love and paused frequently to scan the faces before him, letting the potency of the words penetrate.

Since Tony started his job, Vita had seen him only twice. Once he came to meet her at the front door of the high school to walk her home. "I'm doing this for you," he'd argued then. "I mean, for us. To be together soon. Vita—." He'd had to reach out and pull her back to him as she hurried down the school steps toward the street.

"I have to get home and take over the store now," she'd said, which was partially true. The family always needed her help at some time in that store, even in winter when business was slow.

"Why won't you talk to me?" He'd been working hard, always with the vision of Vita before him and how it would be. "I'm saving my money," he told her. "We can be on our own by spring." As he rushed to keep pace that afternoon, Tony wanted only to convince her of this dream, this possibility within their grasp. "You'll have your diploma and we'll get married." He tried to tease. "We can have our wedding night in Bennet Park."

But she only strode forward, shrugging off his hand and refusing, refusing to be swayed by his fervor, his heat that she could feel even in her layers of wool and Tony in layers of wool and the January temperatures well below freezing. A block from the grocery, she stopped to face him. "Maybe I don't want to marry someone who only pays attention to his own plan. Did you think about that? You did what you wanted to do. It's not what I want."

Tony gripped her wrist so she would not wheel around suddenly and be gone. "You're doing what you want too, Vita. You're finishing school. It will all work out." He knew that it would. "When you're done with school, we'll get married. I'll have money and we can find a place to live together." This was like a prayer to him, like his mother's Hail Mary, something he repeated so often and so surely that nobody, not even Vita in her anger, could convince him otherwise. "We can sleep together," he whispered, although there was no living thing anywhere in sight. He squeezed her arm. "Isn't that what you want too?"

Vita met his eyes, searched his face, roamed the lines of his cheekbones and mouth and tried to remember how they had felt to her in those dark nights together. He was handsome and he loved her. He meant to make her happy. She knew that's what he meant to do.

"I'm alone, Tony," she said. "That's how your plan is working for me. I'm alone."

The weeks apart had not been weeks for Vita, but eras. Christmas. The New Year. After the New Year, Kitty threw herself a birthday party to which Vita went without Tony. Vita's brother, Billy, had a flu that threatened the whole family. A blizzard passed through delaying her father's shipment from Chicago. She'd read two books, done countless algebra problems, baked a cake that had failed to rise in the oven, and she'd cried herself to sleep many nights, missing Tony. And not just Tony, but the way she'd felt when they were together.

Tony knew none of this nor was it remotely true for him. He had not been alone for a minute. He worked harder than he'd imagined men worked, on his feet for twelve hours at a time or more, lifting and shoveling, moving dirt and ore and heavy equipment. He'd been jostled, goaded, razzed, and pushed to work harder and had earned respect for doing just that, for showing the other real men that he was one of them, worthy, reliable, strong. And all that while, through all those difficult shifts at Oliver Mining, he thought of Vita and the way her curls tumbled about and how she felt when wrapped around him. That's what drove and sustained Tony. He was not alone. How could she say she was alone? Weren't they together in every thought? Didn't they live for one another?

"I'm always with you, Vita."

"No," she replied and drew her wrist away from him. "You are not." Then she'd run off to the store and, though he'd started after her, he had not gone inside and she had not turned around to watch him walk into the dusk and home.

That was Vita's first encounter with Tony in the new year. The second was more surprising. It was late morning on a Sunday, a day so cold the religious had to evaluate the wisdom of keeping holy the Sabbath. Vita and her older sister, Rose, sat behind the counter not expecting any business and having an aimless sort of chat about next to nothing. Tony bounded in with great energy, stomping his boots as to warm his feet and slapping his heavy gloves together, his clean face red with cold and heartiness. Behind him the bells jangled wildly. "Ladies," he announced, "does this kindly establishment offer hot beverages?" He grinned and raised his eyebrows into the wool of his knit hat.

Vita's sister hopped off her stool. "My goodness, are you frozen? You look like you're frozen."

"Rose, this is Tony Babić. He was in my class at school."

"Nice to meet you, Tony. I've seen you before. You've come to the store before, haven't you?" Rose glanced over at Vita for acknowledgment, and Tony grinned again, enjoying Rose Marković's confusion and glad to have a secret he shared with Vita.

"Sure," he boomed, "I'm a customer and I'm a classmate." He took off his right glove and pumped Rose's hand.

He was hard to resist. Rattling on about the north wind as he walked the two aisles of the store, Tony plucked items off their shelves with gusto and held them in a jumble in his arms as he continued.

Rose made wide eyes in mock wonder to Vita, who stayed right where she'd been when Tony entered the store. It seemed her legs had gone stiff and still the very second she'd seen his face.

"You asked about a hot beverage," Rose said. "Do you want tea?"

"Wonderful! I would love that, Rose," Tony answered. "I knew I could count on Marković's Grocery, on all of you." He set his purchases down and watched Rose wave in good cheer before running upstairs. "You're so pretty," he said to Vita as soon as they were alone. "I think how pretty you are and wonder if it can be real. But here you are." He threw his arms open. "Here you are."

"It's nice to see you," Vita said. "My sister likes you."

At that Tony sobered and the large good cheer left his face.

"Would you like to see me again soon? We could go to the movies. Sit in the back row," he added with a hopeful smile. "I'd sure like to sit with you over at the State Theater, Vita. Buy you popcorn."

He was trying so hard, but Vita did not know her mind, had no idea how to respond to this confident new rogue version of Tony with his arms open wide and his pockets full of change. Instead of answering him, she asked her own question. "How's work?"

"Hard. Good, I guess. I keep saving my money."

"Not today," Vita commented, scanning his pile of canned fruit and canned fish, boxes of Saltines and chocolates. "You throwing a party or something?"

Tony shook his head and laid out his coins in short stacks on the old counter. "I'd spend any of my money to see you. I even took a chance on facing your dad coming over to the store today."

"I understand," she said, because she thought she did understand. She understood that he continued to be in love with her. She just didn't understand what that meant, where it would take them or—even if she felt the same way anymore.

"Hot tea," Rose called from the doorway. She reached a cup and saucer toward Tony with a satisfied, even proud expression of hospitality. "Should I have brought one for you too, Vita?"

Vita shook her head and both girls, in their plain dresses and store aprons, watched Tony gulp the hot liquid and nod in appreciation. "Thank you," he said. Then none of them said anything. Vita had bagged his groceries and put his money into the register. Rose had gone and returned with his tea which Tony had now finished. He did not know what more to say and neither did Vita or her sister.

After the awkward silence, Tony pulled on his gloves and took up his groceries. "See you again soon," he said.

"See you, Tony," Vita replied with so much regret she thought she'd break down and cry right there. Why did she resist him? She could have had a date to go to a movie with him, felt him next to her in the back row of the State Theater downtown. She could have seen him soon as he had hoped.

"Nice to meet you," Rose said with a girlish wave. "Bye-bye."

The bells jangled again and he was gone, the top of his head dashing past the front window as he went.

"I think he likes you, Vita," Rose commented as she settled herself back on her stool behind the counter. "He looks nice, like a nice guy."

"He works in the mine now."

"So does everyone, Vita. That's why he has money to spend."

"I suppose. I liked it better when I saw him at school though."

"School isn't everything," Rose said defending him. After all, hadn't she left too at the age of sixteen? "Where does it get you, all that homework?"

"Where does leaving get you?" Vita snapped. "Anyway, Pa told me I couldn't go out with Tony. Last summer he said that."

"He did? That's who you were going out with?" Rose stared at her sister. "I never know anything around here." Which wasn't true, of course, because as the oldest and the only one not in school, she knew basically everything that happened in the family. "Pa better get used to us all seeing people. Honestly, Vita. We aren't getting any younger."

That comment, for some reason, made Vita feel worse.

And now it was Valentine's Day and Mr. Dryer continued to read them poetry, his voice rising and setting like the sun itself. *If all the world and love were young, And truth in every shepherd's tongue, These pretty pleasures right me move, To live with thee and be thy love.* The words were the quandary of Vita's own life, the dilemma of loving yet somehow—not enough.

WANT

We didn't have much. That's what I think. What did we have? Something to wear, something to eat, a house full of kids, some chairs and beds, fresh eggs. I look around now and it's hard to believe. Boat parked behind the garage. Closets of clothes. A new car every four, five years. If I want a better lawn mower, I go buy one. Then I fix up the old one and make it go again. Monkey around with the engine, replace this or that, wash the whole thing and stick it in the driveway with a For Sale sign taped to the handle. I've got envelopes of pocket money just selling things I fixed—fans, lamps, mowers. You name it.

Everybody now has things and more things. Houses filled with them, stacked with them. Stores are so big you can't find where the hell you came in or what you wanted in the first place. The stores back then were small, like the Markovićs' store. One-room outfits with the family living in the back or upstairs, running in and out every time the door opened with some customer. Or there were specialty stores, drugstores, department stores. But none of them like these places today. You think you'd walk into any store back then and get lost in the aisles? Think again, I tell you.

Even so, if we had jack squat, we were just like everyone else. Almost nobody had much. I'm not saying we were satisfied or that we wanted for nothing. We wanted all right. I wanted to be a hockey player, drive a car, learn clarinet like Benny Goodman. But we lived too far out for me to be on the hockey team all winter and nobody was about to give me a clarinet or teach me how to play. I did get a car pretty young, a clunker I bought with my own money and hid in the woods. I made that happen on my own.

But Tony never drove a car and maybe he never wanted to. That I cannot say. Keeping an eye on Tony in those days I could tell you what he did want though. Tony wanted one step up. You see a guy combing his hair all the time, reading books, ironing his shirts, dreaming of a girl a mile or so away and you know he wants something better for himself.

And I can tell you all my life I've done like Tony. Keep a comb in my back pocket, shave every day, even twice if I need to, press my pants and iron my own shirts since my wife died, keep my nails trimmed and I look ahead. I look ahead. You want to live to be ninety years and then some, I'm going to tell you here and now you better look ahead. What's the past? A good story or two. Nothing to turn you upside down. Whatever happened, it happened. Tony's life happened. He had a girl, a gift, a dream. Say what you will, that's what he had. As long as he kept his eyes forward he was in good shape, my brother Tony. The trouble comes when you start hanging around in the past, want to catch trains already left the station. That's when things change.

Years later, lots of years later, my younger brother Nikko said well maybe Tony was one of those guys who got depressed for no reason. New research, Nikko said, and shook his head this way and that like he knew everything and all you had to do was ask. But Nikko and Georgie were too young to remember the Tony the rest of us knew.

I asked my sister Margaret once what she thought changed Tony. "Maybe he was too smart for his own good," she said to me. This is the kind of thing Margaret would say. She never got through high school. None of my older sisters did and I can't even tell you why. Petey quit to get married and my brothers dropped out for the war. Other than my baby sister, I'm the only one finished school. Saved my own money for a ring, too, which I'm proud of to this day.

I didn't care much for school, but I finished. So what's that say about me? I'm the guy with a comb in his back pocket who married a woman who read at least five books a week until the day she died. Even the day she died, there was that book open on the kitchen table, book marker in place ready to be continued the next day. Only that time there wasn't a next day. My wife died in a minute. Out to dinner with me at six and hooked up to machines by midnight. That's what I mean about the past. What good does it do to think about it? But my wife was even smarter than Tony. That's the kind of girl I picked after all my goofing around.

I met my wife at the VFW club. Who doesn't know that story by now since we told it a hundred times? She'd been working at the Pentagon under Eisenhower, high security clearance the whole thing. She worked there through the war and after, came home for some kind of surgery, and stayed with her parents to recover. She went to the movies with a friend one night and stopped at the VFW for a drink and there I was. Casanova. Dressed up and dancing the floor. I bought her a drink and so on and so on. She was Italian and I took to that. I spoke pretty decent Italian after the war, working the trains in Italy like I did. I always liked Italians. I play bocce, make wine, all of that. By now I'm probably as much Italian as I am Croatian and anyway, what's the difference? One sea and a few islands.

I liked my in-laws as soon as I met them. It was a different family than my own. Her brothers were businessmen and smart, shrewd even. Her dad owned property, a house here, another over there, and there and there. I offered to help him with things because I could see the old man could grow a garden and make money and everyone liked him around town, but he couldn't fix things for shit. And his sons were worse. Light switches in backwards. One step to the basement over a foot deep and the next one maybe half of that. But the properties were nice and I helped with those properties as long as Mr. and Mrs. were alive. It came easy to me. I do everything tidy, no paint on the floor, no grass under the fence, no rough seams when I weld. I used to tell my kids, if you can't do it well, don't do it. Almost thirty years I helped with those properties, changing windows, painting, mowing, you name it.

Maybe I was not always happy about that. I think my wife thought I did too much, even though they were her parents. But now, thinking about it, I have nothing but respect for that whole bunch. I'm glad I helped like I did. My father-in-law taught me how to make wine and I ate my mother-in-law's food. She was some kind of cook, my mother-in-law, and

I stayed part of a family that took me in like I was one of their own. Johnny this and Johnny that. By then my brothers were going in their own directions, my sisters married, even my baby sister, and here was this small Italian bunch taking me in like one of their own. I had a good life with my wife's family. And they all liked me, I'll tell you that too. One of her nephews came on vacations with us when we were young. A smart kid like Tony. Always an answer, that kind of kid. Went to school for a hundred years and got a good job so he could retire before he was fifty. Nice guy. They're all nice. I love them all.

My sisters Anna and Katie and Helen got married young, but Margaret, no. Margaret spent a life doing housework, mostly for the priests, which she loved. Her own house, size of a dime, was a shrine to Jesus and Mary, let me tell you. Statues and holy cards, rosaries hung on the walls, a crucifix over every piece of furniture blessing the whole works. She married late, a guy who never said much and always knew enough to stay out of the way and go along with her prayers whenever they came at him. Not that I don't have a crucifix over the bed too. My wife hung it there the way they all did, keeps you from dying in your sleep. I held on to pretty much everything my wife left behind. Crucifix over the bed. Perfume bottles in a row on the dressing table, books on shelves everywhere, folded handkerchiefs in the top drawer. Seems hard to see her things there sometimes, but seems like not seeing them would be worse.

I don't think Tony was too smart for his own good, but my sister Margaret might have meant the same thing I mean when I say that he wanted something he didn't find or couldn't name or it didn't find him back. Vita must have loved my brother, all the time they spent together and his hard-earned money buying her sodas, but that could have changed. He could have loved her more than she loved him.

Pete and I poked at him about Vita, watched him pressing those shirts with Ma's iron, followed him half out of the Morris when he went to meet her. But we didn't know. If something started to crush Tony back then, two kid brothers with dirt on their knees were not the ones to figure it out.

Years after, when I worked at that same meat market where Tony worked in high school, I spent time with one of the daughters over there. Natalie Conti was her name, nice looking, sweet. I'd graduated by then and I'd been driving cars for four, five years, so they hired me to deliver meat around town. That's how we did it then. People ordered meat or milk or whatever they needed and guys like me would drive over and deliver. The Contis liked me, I'll tell you that.

I painted their truck, did letters on the side all neat and white—Conti Meats. I added some class to the operation, talked Italian to the customers, *Ciao*, Mrs. Dominica, *come stai oggi?* I'd roll my eyes around, make the ladies laugh.

I slept in the bunkhouse out at their farm, ate with the farmhands and family, and Natalie Conti got a thing for me. And I liked her too. I could say now that I loved her. Love's nothing to hang on to like some one-time deal. I loved lots of people in my life and I'll say that Natalie Conti was one of them.

But after a year in that kind of life, I got a job with U.S. Steel working the trains. There was war overseas by then and the mines started producing again, started getting out of that Depression slump. The Contis were good people and they treated me right, but U.S. Steel paid real money and I could start building seniority. Turned out more important, I got train experience, which the military liked and that saved me from the infantry. Probably saved my life, that first job with U.S. Steel. I didn't know all that then, but I did leave the Contis high and dry. Left the job, the family, the daughter. Everyone thought we'd get married like her older sister Julia, but it wasn't my time. I walked away.

My mother was pretty mad about that and she didn't

used to get mad at me, Ma. I'd say she kind of favored me. I took time for her, that's how it was. I took time for my mother-in-law, too, and drove across the Iron Range a hundred times in later years to visit my sister Margaret in the nursing home. But back then, Ma was not happy with me.

Natalie married the next good-looking guy who came along, a guy who never did right by her. Cheated on her all the time, which everyone knew. I saw him once after the war sitting on a stool at Checco's Bar, hanging all over some girl. Made me sick. I loved her better than that. But I left. And I never cheated on my wife, no matter how many women came around. I don't go for that.

But I didn't do right by Natalie either. She got some crippling disease and died not long after the war. I didn't think about her so much for years, but now I do. Looking out the window here, feet up, I've got lots of time to think and in comes Natalie Conti, all young and sweet and figuring we will get married.

So maybe Vita was like me that way. Maybe she changed and that's why Tony changed. Then again it could have been something else altogether, but who do I ask? A house full of people and it comes down to just me. It's tough, let me tell you. After my last brother died, what I did, I put flowers at the Babić tombstone. It's in the old part of the cemetery now, the ground all sunk around it from more than eighty years of sitting out there in every kind of weather, under five feet of snow or who knows what. I do the planter myself. A spike, a vinca vine, two geraniums, and a petunia. My wife taught me that. I do a planter for her too. And for my in-laws too. Then once a week I drive out and water the whole works. Some days I'm lugging my boat behind. I go fishing on Island Lake or any of those lakes out that direction, Swan or Prairie, then I swing through the cemetery to water the flowers.

I can't even count the questions I have about my family now they're all gone. Ask me why did my parents leave Croatia. How the hell do I know? We were so busy being poor and working hard and grabbing fun at every chance and then the war came and then we all got married and had kids and problems, the mines went on strike in the fifties, then Pa died, then Ma, then Pete, and on down the line, one funeral after the next. I went to every funeral. I'd drive two hundred miles if I had to just to get there, but I'd get there. Because what we had, the Babić family, when all was said and done, what we had was each other.

After supper some winter nights, maybe a blizzard going strong, my brother Petey would pick up his broom and strum it like a guitar, humming away at that thing, and my sister Katie would pull Margaret off her chair to polka around the room and Ma would laugh shy like she did and Pa stomp the beat and there we'd be, having our own good fun all by ourselves with the biggest ore pit in the world a throw from our door and the worries of life out of view.

So whatever Tony's story, whatever it is. That's part of it too.

FIVE

Spring 1929 to Winter 1930

i.

Luka did not see it coming. Maybe some bankers in their carpeted sanctuaries had an inkling, maybe high rollers watching their dividends day by day did as well. But Thursday, October 24th was just like any other workday for Luka, keeping watch, looking for upset, hoping for no upset and listening to the guys he worked with jostle and beef like they always did. If these guys invested their money beyond the local savings and loans, he had no idea, their banter about gains and losses never interested him. Luka still preferred to keep his money in the leather bag his grandfather had made for him. Who was to know how much he had or didn't have? It was his business. That's the way he'd learned to live.

On that Tuesday, Chicago had witnessed a storm to remember, Lake Michigan raging in what the newspaper had called "unprecedented fury," ending in sea walls smashed away, debris scattered everywhere, snow and howling winds at more than fifty miles per hour. Wednesday had been a day of recovery. And then

Thursday, stocks crashed just as the concrete drives had during the storm, one upheaval following the other. Days later, there was a rally. Days after that, a slump to end the rally. The market scare continued, the scare was over, stocks tumbled, stocks went up, a New York banker committed suicide.

It had been a rollicking decade, money was money and the ground they walked was solid. Nobody seemed to anticipate the crash nor have an idea about what was to come in the years that followed. On November 14th, President Hoover cut income taxes by 160 million dollars and both the Republicans and Democrats supported him. A week later he pledged no wage cuts. But Luka was not sure anyone believed anything at that point.

And he had other things on his mind beyond the financial state of the country. Early in the year, when he applied to the Bureau of Investigation in Washington, DC, Luka had been contacted for an interview which happened late spring. He had waited the hot, violent summer for word that he would or would not be hired. At Sacred Heart on Sundays he could not help but pray for his chances, though he knew God disapproved of such self-interest; the priests of his childhood had assured him of that. Still he bowed his head in full and deep concentration to ask for this, this chance to be a federal agent and fight crime at a higher level, to be on a special force that might take down an Al Capone or any of his cohorts. He prayed for his chances just as he prayed for the poor and their struggles, and the sick, the downtrodden, and all those murdered on the streets of the city. As the country's financial problems mounted, he also prayed for revival, for restraint and calm.

"I lost my job," Kata told him after church the first Sunday in December. It was snowing outside, but quietly, and they had stayed to have their customary coffee and sweet after Mass. Kata spoke into her chest, not sure she wanted him to hear what she had just said.

"No! Kata, that's terrible."

"Things are too slow. Maybe they can hire me back in three or four months when business goes back to usual, they said. But my supervisor lost her job too." She tugged at the empty fingers on her glove. "It's the way things are now everyone says."

Luka leaned forward close to her. "What will you do then, Kata?"

Her eyes on him were large and, it seemed to Luka, terrified. "I never thought this would happen."

He felt angry on her behalf. "It's all finance and speculation, banks and big companies. Then hardworking people like you lose their jobs."

"Good thing you're a cop, Luka. Cops never lose their jobs. Especially in Chicago." She nodded knowingly. "Can you imagine what would happen if we had any fewer cops?"

But a week later, Chicago announced that the city planned to cut both fire and police jobs across the board, a move the budget makers said would save the city almost four million dollars. What the outcome would be in fighting crime was another story, of course. Luka kept hoping to hear from the Bureau of

Investigation, to get out of the whole Chicago mess.

Just before Christmas, the city got hit by another storm, a blizzard, which always set people back no matter when. Businesses lost customers, accidents happened, always some poor person— or several—got caught in the blinding snows and died, and here they were in the throes of financial unrest, with jobs being cut in all industries and banks unwilling to lend money, even to the city of Chicago. Police received their last paycheck for many weeks on December 24th. Luka thanked every saint he could name for his savings tucked into that little leather sack he'd had since he was a much younger man. He bought Kata a simple ring set with a small garnet, had the store wrap it for him with a silky red ribbon, and walked with it to her rooming house.

She'd been trying so hard to be solid and unafraid, but it was taking its toll on her, Luka could see that it was. Her eyes looked dark and tired and she had perhaps run out of her favorite lipstick, because her face seemed more pale, less vibrant. Luka asked her to get her coat and hat, that pretty, frosted cake of a hat, so that he could take her out for dinner. They walked in the snow to the Polish restaurant where they had gone for Valentine's Day not so long ago and yet so long ago. And then sitting at a lovely, cloth-covered table in the corner of the room, Luka asked Kata if she'd like to marry him.

He said, "I think we're a good team, Kata. We're alike in so many ways. I think it's right for us to be together." That's what he said, holding her hand across the tiny table. What he did not say was that the daydreams of love he'd had as a young man looked foolish to him in the face of such difficult times, that he'd rather make safe conversation with a sweet and loyal wife than continue imagining a kind of romance that he'd never known anyway. That he wasn't sure anyone ever did know anyway. That he didn't want her to be alone. Or that he didn't want to be alone either.

She cried so hard, like the floodwaters within her had burst wide open. "Oh, Luka, I'm so happy," she said again and again. She rolled the little ring around and around in her hand as if it were the key to heaven. Maybe she thought it was her key to heaven. Luka was so nice, so handsome, so familiar and hard-working and honorable. He was everything she'd ever thought she'd want in a husband.

"I love you so much," she said, her face a smear of tears. "I just can't believe how happy I am."

He nodded and nodded and kept smiling with a new pride and amazement. Women were so interesting! He had no idea that little ring and his solemn proposal would change Kata's whole life right there in the Polish restaurant. He laughed out loud. "I love you, too, Kata," he answered, not knowing what love was or what he felt, but believing it was all for the good no matter what.

They stayed for hours eating pierogis, cabbage rolls, and pork cutlets. They drank wine and then coffee and Luka spared nothing that night when he asked Kata to marry him. They decided they would plan their wedding for the next Valentine's Day, a date which Kata recalled as an anniversary of sorts, the night when they first came to this restaurant and she thought maybe Luka liked her more than she had known. They would talk to the priest at Sacred Heart and see what could be done. They would write to their parents who would all be so pleased to know their child was marrying another Croatian out there across the wild Atlantic in the even wilder country of America.

Luka still had not heard from the Bureau, but he remained hopeful—and in this near-giddy, hopeful state of mind he wrote to Tony Babić to say he was getting married, he planned to be a federal agent to take down big-name criminals, and, despite the country's financial woes, he was fine, he was happy. How are you? he asked Tony. Do you still like working in the mine? Are you making your own plans to marry your girlfriend, Vita, with the most pretty face? How is your mother and the new baby I've never seen? Luka went on and on as if Tony Babić were his younger brother, which he almost thought he was, and would want to hear all this good news from Luka, would be bolstered by good news from afar, from an old friend who cared about Tony.

Come see me soon, Luka wrote at the end of his cheery letter. You are always welcome to come see me, Tony.

Luka's positive outlook was not in keeping with everything happening around him. Crime in Chicago had not lessened with the stock market crash and in mid-January 1930, the city sought to add 5,400 additional police, no matter the budget, in an effort to counter the criminals that operated freely at every level of society, from the elegant set gathered in plush dining rooms to those punching each other in the back alleyways.

In only one week that month, Chicago had endured 192 robberies which killed four people and wounded dozens more. Police Commissioner William Russell decided this was the time to demonstrate what an expanded police force could do to curb crime and ordered a wide net of retaliation unlike anything in the city's history. Cops went everywhere, arresting men in tuxedos in Loop hotels and those at the bottom of the rung in gambling joints, they went into every neighborhood in the city. On a single day 2,694 criminals were rounded up and thrown in jail. Luka was part of all this, this just and overdue wave against crime, and it made him feel purposeful and part of something that mattered.

But that was not the last of it. Two weeks later, on February 10th, hundreds more gangsters were seized and jailed to wait out their time before a grand jury, a move meant to curb the "gun terrorists" on the streets of Chicago.

"Take the guns away from these assholes," was what Luka heard from his fellow policemen. "You give a maniac a gun and whaddya think is going to happen?"

Luka agreed completely, he could not agree more.

But many things happened that day in many places.

The letter didn't arrive for several weeks. He'd married Kata by then and had mail from Croatia to congratulate him. His mother sent a carved crucifix to hang over their bed and his father sent gold coins wrapped in paper, buried in fold upon fold with incredible determination.

Seeing a letter from Margaret Babić didn't alarm Luka, but maybe his heart skipped a beat or two. He'd never heard from Margaret before. She had been so young when he left the Iron Range, and he wasn't quite sure if she was the oldest sister so responsible or the talkative younger sister always being shushed. She was writing with news of Tony. She thought Luka should know. It happened February 10th, she said, as if it were important for Luka to know the exact day.

He would always remember. That week before he got married and the city of Chicago rounded up hundreds of men with their guns. Far away on the Iron Range of Minnesota, Tony Babić lost his grasp, this news shaking the way Luka thought of the world, the story staying with him like a scar that pulls and flares and itches ever after.

ii.

All the Markovićs came to Vita's high school graduation. Her father sat in a velvet auditorium seat feeling like a king, how kings lived, he thought, in such ornate glory, domed ceiling and balconies, thick carpet and mirrored doors. Here he was, waiting for his daughter to march by in her graduation gown and hat, on her way to a diploma, organ music blasting to beckon the chariots onward.

It may have been the first time in George Marković's life when he felt humbled. Not challenged or overwhelmed as he'd been at more times than he cared to remember, but humbled by the grandeur of this building his community owned. Sure, the mining company had paid for it. But then the town's people kept the mining companies in business with hard work and sacrifice, with their willingness to move the whole damn place a mile down the road. So, this school, with all its gild and polish, was theirs. That's what George Marković thought.

"Vita!" Billy arched tall, craning to get a full view of his sister coming down the aisle. "There she is, Ma!" he said again, claiming her, this sister who was doing what he knew he would do as well. He would stay in school until he finished and wear a gown like Vita was wearing and a silly flat hat like that too. He could hardly stay still, no matter what the speakers had to say, their high ideals, our nation, our freedoms, our plenty, and the music lifting everyone upward. Billy absorbed it all. Like incense, a heady smoke he breathed in and allowed to become part of him.

When the graduates crossed the stage, Vita face-flushed and grown, George Marković could not stop the tears that fell and dripped to the collar of his brown serge suit. He never had this dream of school the way Vita did. He'd learned how to read, write, and do numbers. He'd learned as a boy in Croatia and again as a young man in America, catching on quickly to whatever he needed to survive and succeed, and that was enough for any man as far as he was concerned.

When the ceremony was over, George ushered his family along, his hands on their backs to guide them, nodding graciously to people he recognized in the slow line moving out of the auditorium and into the wide tiled hallway. He pulled his five-foot-five frame as tall as possible, tipped his chin upward and smiled with dignity and control, though he wanted to leap about, light a cigar, and shout to high heaven.

His wife spotted Vita ahead of them in the throng of people, her hat removed and curls tumbling.

"Who's she talking to, Billy? Who's that boy talking to Vita?"

Billy stood on his toes to see what his mother was seeing. Vita, just ahead of her family, focused happily on a classmate who was reaching down to move a stray wisp of hair off her forehead.

"Michael Brennan," he told his mother.

"He's Irish?"

"I don't know, Ma. He plays hockey. Kids like him."

Mrs. Marković took in the boy's fine features, freckles and sandy, smoothed hair. "I never heard of that family."

"Lots of people we don't know, Ma. Not everyone buys groceries in Brooklyn." Billy felt he had responsibility to continually remind his family of the larger world, even in this small mining town. All people did not go to one of the Catholic churches or buy sausages from George Marković or even know someone they knew.

"You don't have to tell me that," his mother said with a small swat at him. This boy up ahead flirting with her daughter looked like the kind of nice boy most mothers would welcome. Maybe she should welcome him, too, and be pleased that Vita, at age eighteen, had suitors and now a high school diploma and some kind of future beyond Marković's Grocery.

But this Irish boy by the name of Brennan was not Tony Babić whose parents came from Brusane and belonged to the Croatian Union and who had been crazy about Vita for a very long time. Her husband hadn't favored him, but who would George have favored? These old bohunk men thought they owned their daughters. That's what they thought. Then when the girls were twenty and unmarried like Vita's sister Rose, they were labeled old maids and forgotten. So why should a mother care if it was Tony Babić or Michael Brennan or any healthy, decent boy who would marry Vita and get her going on her own family? Still. It was hard to top Tony Babić.

At their home, the Markovićs held a party in the backyard with two tables of food and another of drinks. George's cousin Vlado played his accordion and sang, and anyone who could stand on two feet—from toddlers to old men—danced polkas around the yard. The first in their extended family to graduate from high school, Vita seemed a new specimen to all the relatives at the party. They wanted to see what a high school graduate looked like.

After dancing with Vita, her Aunt Lo remarked to her husband, "Vita seems the same to me."

"What do you think, Lo? Going to school means you don't go to the toilet no more?"

"Going to school means you don't talk like a toilet, you."

Her husband threw his head back and laughed, his mouth half empty of teeth and his merriment large. "Not going to school means you still talk all the time though, eh?"

George Marković strode from one cluster of relatives to another, pride puffing his chest out full as a boxer.

For Vita, the night had been everything she'd wanted, and now here she was in the circle of family and well-wishers with some kind of future before her, she was sure of it. And Michael Brennan? She hadn't known Michael Brennan, hadn't paid attention or noticed him among the many accomplished boys in her class.

She had thought only about Tony for so long. Even when he left school and she was alone, she continued to remember. Even when she saw him now and then, she did not accept their current situation. She became someone only remembering, no different than dreams, these gauzy thoughts of what happened or might happen.

Tony loved her, she knew he did—and she liked to think she'd love him again, in the summer on their picnic table maybe. Or they'd get married like he always said, though something in that dream didn't take hold for her anymore.

Kitty had endless dreams of marriage, from the bed she'd share to the flowers she'd plant by the kitchen door. She couldn't talk enough about marriage. What God had put together would last joyfully forever through embraces and children, under full moons and the northern sky. So her friend followed her favorite boys, organized encounters, moved along in her own way not knowing that no matter the face of love, its heart would hold contradictions and skip full beats. But at least Kitty attached some strategy to her wanting. Vita just floated on what was and might be.

Until now.

When Michael Brennan came up to her after graduation and his hand touched her skin, Vita flew to him as a wild bird to its mate.

"Michael Brennan's a nice guy," Billy remarked to Vita at the party in his knowing way, keeping track as he did.

"Do his friends call him Mike?"

Billy's mouth puckered in thought. "Now that's something I do not know."

"You really don't know? I asked my brother a question he cannot answer?"

"Maybe they call him Mikey the way people do. Like Bobby, Joey, Jimmy, Billy."

"He doesn't seem like a Mikey."

"More like a Mike?"

Vita grinned and bumped up against her brother. "More like a Michael Brennan."

Then to her surprise the very same arrived on his own to the Markovićs' party, just as their relatives were wandering off in different directions home. He didn't consider whether he belonged or not. The Markovićs had a store, after all, used to people coming and going. He saw the backyard activity and paused, searched, then gravitated further into the gathering, hands in his coat pocket and hat cocked just so. Michael Brennan was not one to hesitate or fret. He'd been fostered by a tangled family of good-humored survivors who took their luck and thanked the Lord for whatever partialities they received. Michael had surely been one of the Lord's partialities—intelligent, kind, able. He moved with grace and genuflected in such an easy swoop to the floor that his mother and her sisters were convinced he was meant to be a priest.

Michael Brennan wasn't planning any particular future with Vita, but he was interested in her. He sensed in Vita Marković something of himself—she held to the moment, was attractive and vibrant but without designs, without calculation. When he found her in the thinning group of well-wishers in her yard, she smiled as readily as he did. "Hello," she greeted him, as though he had been bound to show up there at some point.

"Hello, Vita," he said in return.

iii.

Tony had no idea. The day Vita graduated high school, he did a double shift, clocking in at seven in the morning and staggering home just after eleven that night with enough dirt on his face that he had to scrub it twice just to shave. He hadn't seen Vita in weeks and the last time he did, he was so certain that she loved him, he forgot to worry. He'd saved more than one hundred dollars in his six months of work. He had a bank account at First Federal in his name. One day when he didn't have to be at work until three in the afternoon, he walked all over town hoping to find For Rent signs. All this fueled his hope for life with Vita after she graduated.

He needed to think that way. Work was hard as Jocco had warned him and as every boarder had also warned him. The big old mine swallowed them up the minute their boots touched its ground. As a new guy with no trade, Tony had to take whatever came his way from scrubbing the plant floors to shoveling pounds of ore. The physical burden was one thing for sure, but the lack of independence felt worse. He had no say. He had no power. He did what he was told to do and no one cared to hear his opinions. How they might work faster, waste less time, be better motivated. He was an eighteen-year-old who knew which European countries bordered which and the major battles of the Civil War. No one cared. Tony Babić worked from the bottom of the heap.

And he worked so many hours he had gradually, over the months, come to regard Vita as his muse, his phantom love. She was promise and memory and illusion. She was everything he wanted. But most of the time, she was not real. He didn't have time to date her as before. She was often in school when he was off work. They had almost no time of their own. They had no place of their own.

He didn't mind living with the dream. He believed she lived with it too. How could she not be? They were bonded by an intimacy neither of them had ever known with another being.

"You see Vita?" His mother asked him that these days. "You see Vita, Tony?" She'd nod as she asked. Ma had her longings, too, he supposed. For him to have a Croatian wife or for her first son to live down the road at the Morris or for the worry of a mother's heart to subside. She had been upset when he left school. Now what did she know, Marie Babić and her rosary beads, her mumbled prayers to the Mother of God?

"Sure, Ma," Tony answered. He'd nod too. All in agreement, all together. Tony and Vita.

His sister Margaret did not tell their mother she'd just seen Vita on a downtown street holding hands with a boy she did not recognize, a boy who walked with a lighthearted sway that Tony had never had, that maybe nobody in the Babić family ever had.

But Margaret did tell this to Tony. She carried the image around in heavy consideration before she decided that her brother could not compete for Vita's love if he didn't know there was competition. She chose her night and waited up for him to come home from the late shift. Poured him a glass of Jocco's whiskey. She thought to pour herself one, too, just to give her courage, but she had never liked the taste of whiskey. Or any liquor really.

She wanted Tony to sit with her at the table and sip that whiskey while she presented her news. But Tony stomped in exhausted, set his lunch pail down, took up the glass and downed it on the spot. "Thanks," he said and bent to unlace his boots. He hadn't looked at Margaret, let alone wondered why she was there at that hour pouring whiskey. Margaret, of all people in the household.

"I saw Vita walking with a guy downtown," she blurted. "I mean, together."

Tony stopped what he was doing to straighten and meet his sister eye to eye. "When?"

"A couple nights ago. Anna and I went out for a while."

"Did she see you?"

Margaret was not understanding his reaction. "No. We were behind them."

"So maybe it wasn't Vita."

"It was," Margaret said. "I can recognize Vita Marković when I see her, Tony. I thought you'd want to know."

"But you waited two days?" He glared at her.

"You're always at work, Tony. I stayed up tonight on purpose to tell you and now you get mad at me? I didn't do anything wrong."

"You never do anything wrong, Margaret. What would God say if you did?" He went to work on his other boot and Margaret rose from the table.

"If this is your behavior, no wonder Vita's walking around with someone else. He looked like a nice guy, too, if you ask me."

But Tony did not ask her and felt relieved when she huffed emphatically and left the room without another word. Mostly he didn't believe she'd really seen Vita, though he realized that Vita did have a distinct look with those curls of hers. But Margaret and Anna had been behind her, Margaret said. Tired as he was, Tony wanted nothing more than to hike around the Hull Rust to Marković's Grocery, knock on the door, and ask to see Vita. He wanted to find out the truth for himself.

Yet he couldn't, he wouldn't, because old man Marković would ban him forever if he showed up at this hour of the night. Also, he smelled bad and looked worse. He set his boots by the door, washed in the sink, and went to bed, though his mind would not let him sleep. His visions of Vita now had this other person, this guy Margaret thought she saw, this friendly guy who had time to wander around town on a summer night the way Tony used to do. He saw it all too clearly. The more he worked to squint the image out of his mind, the more stubbornly it remained, fused in his memory as though it had been Tony himself at Vita's side, looking friendly, touching up against her arm, being proud and near dizzy with desire.

He could not relax, could not let go. Lucky he could breathe, the feelings within him were so large, a kind of ore pit in his own heart, he thought. An ore pit so huge he could not circumvent it.

At some point, he heard his mother in the kitchen starting her bread. He half-listened as others in the family came to life, rustling, dressing, scraping chairs, drawing water. The door slammed more than once and two boarders argued in words he couldn't figure. Maybe he finally slept. He thought he did, because when he sat up the house had a midmorning hum and the image of Vita with another guy had become slightly frayed and faint, less likely to be true.

He didn't have to work until three that afternoon, so without detailing a plan, dressed in a shirt he'd ironed exactly, combed his hair such that the natural waves held in place, and he headed over to see Vita.

He had visited the store only once back in the winter when Vita's sister Rose gave him tea. Otherwise he had only been there early in their romance, before George Marković ruled him away. Since then, he'd become a man. He'd found love and understood the heat of intimacy. He'd put away his books and papers and gone to work. He worked with men and got paid as a man and at the end of the day, he assessed what he'd accomplished in a man's world. He was no longer a schoolboy to be shooed off by a protective father. He was ready to go toe to toe with Vita's father if he had to.

But when he stepped into the grocery and heard the familiar bells chiming over the door, he found only Vita behind the counter, unpacking boxes of cookies into glass bulk jars. She started to smile, but seeing that her customer was Tony Babić, the smile shifted to concern. The muscles around her mouth tightened and he caught it. She was not happy that he'd come. For whatever reason, she wished he'd been some neighbor coming by for a pound of lard or the like.

"Hi, Tony. I'm surprised to see you." She fumbled to move her project aside, still trying to smile.

"Yeah, I don't work for a while and I was missing you." He had moved inside as far as the counter's edge and there he remained. "God, it's good to see your face." He wanted to reach out and draw her near, but there was no invitation to do this. The counter seemed larger than he remembered, filling all the space between them. He looked for a sign, any indication that they were lovers, that she still wanted him and missed him. He kept his eyes riveted on her, searching for that sign.

"I'm free tomorrow too," he said. "If you'd like to go for ice cream or lunch or something. We could go to the park. I sure miss going to the park with you."

She smiled in a kind way. "Want a cookie? A wafer or something?"

He shook his head, then changed his mind and put out a hand, but his eyes never left her face. "I could try to get a night off." He glanced anxiously around the store before he leaned in closer. "I've saved money for us, Vita. We need to talk. Make plans. We can make plans now. There's a garage apartment for rent over on Third Avenue West. We could afford that, a little garage apartment for the two of us."

Saying this gave him a boost. Just imagining being with Vita in that garage apartment gave him a boost. "Would you like a ring? Should I ask your dad if I can marry you?"

Somewhere in the middle of his questions, she began to shake her head back and forth and back and forth. And then she said, "No, Tony. I don't want you to ask my father. It's not time. I mean, for you and me. We don't see each other. It's different." She clearly hated everything she was saying.

"I'm working for you and me, Vita."

Now her eyes met his with a different kind of sureness. "I never wanted you to do that. I told you in December I didn't want you to do that. Now it's different. We went different ways."

It was as if she'd never said any of this before to Tony. As though someone had just announced to him that the sun rose in the west or the mines had run out of ore or birds no longer sang.

"You don't love me anymore?" His voice came so low she could not quite hear his words.

"What?"

He did not repeat himself. "I love you," he said instead. "I always will. We were meant to be together, Vita. Think of how we've always been. How it's been with us."

She gave a barely perceptible nod and then they both stayed still. "It's just not the time now," Vita said again. "It's summer," she added, as if that meant anything at all.

"Will you go out with me tomorrow?"

"I can't," she answered. But she did not say why.

"If I got off Saturday night, could we go to the park? See if our picnic table's still there." He chuckled like the table might have walked off to some other place and Vita tried to smile.

"I don't think it will work," she answered. "Maybe later. Maybe at the end of July."

Vita Marković was a kind person who was no longer in love. She had held on to the idea of her and Tony not knowing what she really felt or where it would go. All the remembering consumed her until that night when she graduated from high school and became her own person. Michael Brennan appeared like the Archangel himself and fixed her curls, his eyes easy and open.

She did not know what to say or what to do or why she did not feel the thrill she'd felt not even one year before or even three months before. She wanted Tony to go away so she would not have to feel so bad, would not have to fumble and lie and watch herself breaking another person's heart. "Let's go out at the end of July then," she said to rescue them both.

Tony grinned. "So let's say the last Saturday in July?"

"Yes, Tony. Let's say that then."

He did not leave, but stayed another minute, wanting to say more. "Please think about me, Vita," he said to her. "I think about you every day. I know we'll be happy. Do you believe me?"

She kept her face in the same stiff smile. "I guess I better get back to work now, Tony. You know how it is to work."

He reached across the counter and squeezed her arm, felt her smooth skin and caught the scent of her soap or hair or whatever it was he always associated with Vita. "You look beautiful," he said as he left. When the door closed behind him, Vita exhaled the breath she'd been holding within her since Tony had arrived.

His shirt damp with sweat, but still clean white, Tony headed to the Morris encouraged. The fact that Vita had hesitated, that she had told him this wasn't the time for them and not to ask her father if he could marry her had blurred and nearly disappeared from his thinking. He had a date to see her again, that's what he was thinking. The last Saturday in July. He would see her and it would be as it was. He knew he was scheduled to work, but he'd pay someone to take his shift if he had to. He'd pay double time just to go out with Vita again.

Almost home, Tony realized he'd forgotten to congratulate Vita on her graduation.

He'd just plain forgotten.

iv.

It was never going to happen. That's what Vita decided.

"I don't understand why I feel this way," she confided to Kitty.

Her friend came by often that summer to hang around the grocery, which she thought a more likely place to see and be seen than sitting at home. She worked at night waitressing in the hotel dining room and loved telling Vita her stories of the rich and famous in town who came to the Androy Hotel to drink and dine.

"Last year I would have traded the moon for Tony Babić. Now I don't know what to do. If we go out, he will expect me to be the girlfriend I was, but I'm not that anymore. I threw away all his notes."

"Don't ask me." Kitty threw up her hands dramatically. "I'd go out with him. But maybe if I were you, I wouldn't go out with him."

"Why do you say that?"

"I don't know. Seems like you're somewhere else now."

A customer came by just then and Kitty sauntered off outside. By the time Vita missed her, Kitty was long gone. But not her words. Wherever Vita was that summer of 1929, a high school graduate, a pretty, spirited girl gaining confidence, whatever, she was not Tony Babić's girlfriend any longer and she didn't choose to be.

She thought this through as though it were a life and death matter, then she dug around to find leftover paper from school and she wrote. *Dear Tony,* her letter began, *I will not be able to go out with you later in July. I am thinking about my life and what I will do next. I'm not ready to be married,* she went on, *and do not want to mislead you in any way. You're a good person. I'm glad to have known you so well. We had a good time together. Thank you, Tony.*

She wanted to be certain he understood her absolute intent to end their relationship. So she added, *I hope you find a girl to love you as you deserve.* That was it. She signed it simply Vita.

The next day she folded the letter precisely into one of her father's business envelopes, addressed it to Tony Babić care of the Morris Location, and walked with it to the post office. Maybe it wasn't the most courageous way to say goodbye or the most considerate. But it was the most direct. And now it was done. The ink was on the page and the message and her signature. She tried not to think of it further or to imagine what Tony would do when he read it. He was a sensible person, she assured herself, a man now with a job and money saved. He would know to move on. She hoped he would know to move on and not misconstrue what she had said.

After a few days, Vita began to forget the exact words she'd written and to question their clarity and to doubt her insistence and to agitate more and more about what would happen next. For more than a week she did not leave the grocery. She made up excuses to Michael Brennan when he stopped by with his huge grin and hair flopping onto his forehead. She made up other excuses to Kitty and to her sister Rose and to her brother who hoped she'd go with him to watch a baseball game in the park.

"What, Vita?" her mother said after she heard Vita telling Billy she needed to wash out some personal items. "What's so important to wash tonight?"

"Stockings and things," Vita replied in her best high-and-mighty voice. She tried to ignore her mother's gaze. "Why are you looking at me like that, Ma? I just don't want to go to the park. Or anywhere right now."

"That's new, Vita. For you, I've got to say, that's new. You want to help me make apple jelly then?"

Vita hated doing preserves, a hot slow process, steam kinking her hair and boiling water splashing up to burn her hands. "Ma, I just want to finish down here, wash some underthings and read a book."

Her mother did not relent. "Life's out that door, Vita, not in books—let alone laundry." She left Vita and went upstairs to make the apple jelly herself. Unlike her daughter, Mrs. Marković enjoyed making any kind of preserve, from pickles to cherries.

The routine steadied her, the steam cleared her mind and at the end, she had colorful glass jars on the shelf.

When the children were small, she thought it was the challenging time of motherhood—teaching them all the essentials of dressing, manners, and some element of goodness, industriousness, and respect. It was endless what mothers had to impart to their young. Now that phase of life was over and how surprised she continued to be that mothering did not get easier. Her children's lives had grown larger and more their own. She had less say, less influence. They didn't tell her the real truth, like Vita and the underwear. She had two unmarried daughters over eighteen and she had no idea what they were thinking or how to protect them anymore.

Mrs. Marković had known George since they were kids in Croatia. He hadn't been her first choice, but her first choice had emigrated earlier and she'd lost track of him. And then there was George, a neighbor and family friend, always determined to have his way, which at the time included her. Now they'd made this whole life, so what was there to think about? Not the first love or what might have happened if and where. Maybe the same would be true for her daughters. They'd find their ways, whatever that was.

Vita continued making up excuses to stay home until the last Saturday of July had come and gone. There had been no word from Tony—which is what she had hoped—but now that it was so, it made her uneasy in the way of forest animals smelling a storm, sensing it in their nerve endings, in the very pulse of their bodies. To her, Tony had become someone else, not that smart boy who played on the team and whose hands held such heat he could warm her in a second or sometimes before he even touched her, that heat of fire or sun that was the Tony she had loved so truly. Now he did not hear her. And he no longer knew her.

She said nothing to anyone. She said nothing at all about Tony and when his name came her way, she dodged the reference as quickly as she could. After a while her sisters, her mother, Billy, and Kitty all quit mentioning him, as though every one of them understood something was more amiss now than it had been in the earlier months of the year when Vita and Tony didn't date, those months when Tony had been absent. Tony wasn't just absent in Vita's life now. It seemed he had been completely erased.

For Tony, however, Vita was not erased from his life, at least not from his inner life. He'd read her letter only twice, once in anticipation and a second time to assure himself of what he'd read the first time. Then he'd done what he used to do with her folded, secret notes passed in the halls at school. He dropped it into the hot fire of his mother's stove and watched it turn from white to orange fury and finally black ash. She hadn't said that she didn't love him. But she said she hoped he'd find a girl he deserved. She used the past tense "glad I have known you" like he was some stranger that passed through town and onward.

When Tony was a boy roaming the shrubs and new growth surrounding the Hull Rust, he found a baby bird huddled in the grass. The little thing met him eye to eye and so he picked it up. Carefully holding its wings to its sides, he set it on the skinny limb of a nearby poplar. "Can you fly?" he asked. The little thing blinked and settled further into itself, and after a few minutes, Tony continued on his solitary ramblings. He picked a few wild strawberries that afternoon and brought a handful back to the bird, as though a bit of sustenance would fix whatever was wrong. But the bird was no longer there. Not on the ground near the poplar nor anywhere that he could see.

Now Vita Marković thought Tony was that bird. Her letter set him on a branch and willed him to fly away. That's what he thought for the rest of July and early August and his heart ached and if he thought too long or hard, his head ached as well. Then he began to harbor notions that the long-ago baby bird had never survived, though he could not bear to imagine what might have happened to it. He drifted away from the possibility of freedom to a darker place of loss and dread. He woke at night sometimes then in so much sweat that all the bedding was wet as rain. He took on any number of hours at work just to hold off thinking.

What would become of him without Vita? She'd been his dream for so long, the prettiest girl he'd known or seen. "You're a good person," she'd written. "Thank you," she'd said. So then he had to wonder what was missing and why she was setting him free, if he was a good person and she was glad to know him. What else had she said? He circled this constantly but had no letter to consult. What had she said?

And then as he sat with some older miners taking a break at work, drinking his mother's thin tea out of a thermos, it came to him like a lightning bolt, just that sudden and true. The guy next to him made a comment about marriage, like the guys often did, the wife this and the wife that and Vita's words in ink on the page came right back to him, saying, "I'm not ready to be married." He shuddered enough to jiggle his tea such that the guys around him laughed out loud. "Geesuz, Tony, you're too young to have a stroke."

It wasn't that she didn't want to marry him. She wasn't ready! Not ready to marry anyone. She would change her mind in time and he could wait. He might even change her mind. "Find a girl you deserve," she had written. She was the girl he deserved. He'd already found her. Vita, oh Vita. The heaviness which had consumed him for how many months dissipated. She wasn't ready, but she'd get ready soon enough now that she was out of school. She'd find her way back to him. He felt certain again that the bird he'd placed in the poplar had flown far and high, had lifted up and soared. He concentrated on what he was doing and hoped for what would come. The leaves dropped in vivid color, the grasses turned brown, the dawn came later and later, and the sun set early. Those there on the Iron Range that late October of 1929 had no more prescience than anyone else in the country. They worked, they spent, they rolled along like those smooth logs the mining company had used to haul the town from north to south.

When they read the newspaper's account of wild happenings at the New York Stock Exchange, it was a topic, especially among the men, in the way that national news tended to be one topic after another—political doings, tragic accidents, one event or another happening far away from them. Investors dropped 2,600,000 shares of any and everything into the pit before the day's closing on October 24th, U.S. Steel included. But in Tony's world, it was not yet much of anything. Their local paper reported only the rallies. That was what their readers wanted to know.

v.

Tony was one of the newest guys hired at Oliver Mining, not even a year on the job, and so part of the first wave let go. It was nothing personal, the foreman made clear, his eyes down and Tony's eyes down, the red dirt the only thing between them. Still it was swift and, in its way, incredible. He'd left school to be a miner. Mining made him a man, and so he collected his last paycheck and went back to the Morris not knowing what he was. He even lived in a mining location. It's what made life on the Mesabi Iron Range. Iron ore. Steel. That was it.

At home, Jocco said, "The jobs'll come back soon, Tony. You got your name in now." He'd cleared the phlegm deep in his throat, stared hard. "We'll get you back." But even as he said this, Tony sensed the truth. His father was scared. They lived off the Hull Rust. Jocco had nine kids under his roof, and if more men lost jobs, Marie would lose her boarders and the added income from those boarders. Jocco didn't fear for his own job. He was a pioneer. But his wages might be cut. Miners might strike. Maybe it would blow past, Jocco considered, though once the dark cloud of trouble rolled in, there was no telling where it would hover nor what tempests it would bring. The older man dug into the cupboard for his whiskey and kept pouring out glasses for himself and Tony until they could see the bottom of the bottle.

The next morning Tony walked to town. He returned to the meat market to see if they could use him. After he'd left to work in the mine, they'd brought in someone's cousin new from Italy. Now when he told them the mines were cutting men, he saw their collective worry. As went the mines, so went the town. Sorry, Tony, the owner's wife said. Sorry, Tony, her husband said to him twice. They wrapped up a couple of ham hocks for him to take home to his mother and watched Tony hunch along down the street not looking like the boy they'd hired two years before.

"Jesus, help us," the old man said to his wife, and he meant it.

Tony walked the business district all day looking for Help Wanted signs and stopping in a few stores to inquire anyway. It was as though the town had gone into shock when the stock market crashed, had frozen in time and was now hanging on to old dreams hard. Everyone smiled when he walked in the door with possibly two bits to spend, then became instantly anxious when he asked about work.

It was late November. Midafternoon the snow started, a sharp, sleety mix that pelted his face as he headed north to home. He hadn't thought of Vita all day. He had crossed the street that led past her house without a thought. The snow against his skin hurt and the light of day was diminishing to a low darkness with no stars or moon.

Maybe that was the night his angry visions began. Not visions really, not in any enlightened way, but disturbing scenes like clips from a movie or those newsreels they ran before the movie started—the ones jerky with action and unrecognizable people, soldiers in Germany or some queen waving in a parade—odd images all out of context, alien and foreboding. He woke in the mornings exhausted and disturbed, trying not to count the negative numbers of his life just then. No job, no Vita, no school. Maybe no chance to have the life he thought he would have. No future.

For a time, his mother and sisters gave him space in the house and found projects for him. He fixed two wooden chairs and built another, and for the time it took to do this, he had purpose and stayed calm. One sunny afternoon, he took the gun off its hook by the door and left for the surrounding woods to shoot a couple of rabbits, which he skinned and gave over to his mother for a stew. But there was an awkward quiet in the room when Tony was there. His mother prayed louder. His sister Margaret, who had dropped out of school by then, glanced at him constantly as though he could, at any minute, break into a million pieces.

He said nothing of Vita Marković and tried not to think of her too often. His ideas for the two of them faltered now that he had no job and nothing to offer. Even if Vita decided she was ready to get married and saw him in the old way, that loving, teasing, wide-eyed way, what of it? These days his thoughts of Vita Marković ran in circles, like a dog chasing its tail. He did not wonder what she was doing in her life or if the stock market ups and downs had affected Marković's Grocery or what had become of the boy his sisters had seen her walking with that summer. She'd ceased to be fully flesh for so long. It seemed the love of his life had been recreated in gossamer and light, everlasting like the angels he'd learned about as a child. His angel, but far from his grasp.

Christmas came despite his misfortunes. They were down three boarders by then and two others traveled to visit families in nearby states, leaving the table less jolly in general. Still the Babić family had five small children with their anticipation of festivity, their loud voices and funny antics. Tony's older sisters and mother baked sweets that they rarely had in the house and cooked up a feast with a turkey Jocco got from a friend on the job. They sang some songs and clapped and stomped their feet to show a good time. On Christmas morning, they all made the hike into town to church, the older kids taking turns carrying the baby.

This was the blur of the holiday to Tony whose hope and good sense were wavering more and more by the day. His nights troubling. His fury heightening. He'd always worked hard and done the right thing. He'd been a good student. He'd taken every lousy shift and task thrown his way at the Oliver. He'd loved Vita with respect and kindness, he thought, ironed his shirts to look nice for her, held to her father's unfair limits, offered everything he had and would have. There was no reason for life to have dealt him these negations. His mother prayed constantly. Weren't her prayers worth something?

A certain tangible hold on what was and what should be now eluded Tony. He didn't know. He couldn't see. What had happened to him wasn't right or fair.

"I'm going to Chicago, Ma," he pronounced in early January. "I'll get a job in Chicago. Luka can help me." This notion revived him and so Marie Babić said nothing to him about the violence in Chicago and Jocco said nothing about the unemployment mounting in every part of the country. If his son wanted to take his dwindling stash of earnings and try to find work in Chicago, then that was his choice. At this point, Jocco had worries enough of his own and not nearly enough liquor in his cupboard to hold them at bay.

It was uncanny then that two days later Tony received a letter from Luka, who said he planned to marry the woman he'd met at the Croatian church. He didn't say exactly when, but Tony got the idea it would be soon, that this letter was an announcement of sorts. Luka wrote that he was fine, he was happy, he had applied to be a federal agent and had not been too hurt by the financial crisis though he'd lost some pay. The city hadn't been able to pay the cops for a few weeks, he said, but life goes on, right Tony? That's what Luka said. He asked if Tony would marry his pretty girlfriend Vita. Tony liked that sentence. He liked having Vita's name connected to his future in a letter from a guy like Luka. A guy who fought crime like Luka. For just those few minutes reading the letter, Tony felt part of the world of men again, recognized as a man holding a letter from a Chicago cop who asked about Vita and marriage. He wanted to know about Tony's job, too, asked after his mother and baby sister.

"How's Luka?" His mother's eyes were searching, her distrust of Chicago larger even than her affection for the Croatian cop.

"He's getting married," Tony reported and gave her the rest of the news in the letter.

"What's her name?" Marie Babić wanted to think of people by name, something clear like that, who was who.

"Kata."

"Ha," his mother chuckled, liking that name. She knew girls named Kata. Maybe this one sang well or prayed loudly or knit lacy shawls like other Katas she had known.

Tony folded the letter into the pocket of his shirt. He couldn't go to Chicago now, even though Luka had said to visit anytime. He couldn't barge into Luka's new married life. He didn't want to answer the letter either, for what would he say to match Luka's happiness. The shame of his situation came on him so that, for a split second, he seemed to be blind. The room went black and his mother, shuffling from table to stove, disappeared from sight. When she and the rest of the room around her returned to him, Tony's entire body was trembling.

He moved slowly toward a chair at the table. "Ma, you got some tea for me?" He watched her pour from her old tin pot, drizzle in honey, add milk, and set it before him. If she noticed his condition, she didn't say. Better leave men to sort themselves, she'd learned all those years of Jocco and the boarders. Make tea or soup, slice a hunk of bread and leave them to the concerns they'd never share anyway. Tony heard the muttered prayers she said for him as she worked. Hail Mary, Mother of God. Marie Babić spent half her days with Mary, the Mother of God. They were on close terms, Tony knew, and his own weak prayer was that Mary would bequest at least some of what his mother asked.

Nothing got better the next week or the next. Without fuss or fanfare, U.S. Steel continued to cut men even as the newspapers reported financial rallies, tax cuts and the like. Jocco drank more. Whatever this ride, it would not be over soon.

Late in January, Tony took to walking the street near Marković's Grocery. He didn't turn the corner to go directly past and he didn't linger, but he walked by and looked hard at the windows as if he could see inside. Once in early evening when the lights were on, he saw Vita's sister Rose and her mother talking behind the counter. He didn't see that there were any customers in the store and he didn't see Vita.

In school, Tony had done well in mathematics. The exactness of numbers steadied him back then because once a problem worked out, once he'd found x or y and checked his calculations, then there was no dispute. What was—was. Four and six added together would never be other than ten, and so now he tried to calculate his life this way. If he got a job, then he'd have something to offer Vita again. If Vita found herself ready to marry, then he would be there for her. He spun out these possibilities unceasingly. Feeding the animals, mending floorboards, walking to town. He tried working the math constantly, but no matter the calculation, he always came back to zero. No matter how a person added, multiplied, or divided zero, that's all he'd ever get.

Finally he went back to Marković's Grocery, walked to the door, and pulled it open without allowing himself to retreat. The bells chimed above him. Vita stood alone and he saw, before his eyes even focused on her, how her body stiffened. He saw the worry like a thick, invisible wall between them and her pretty, frozen face peering at him over the wall. "Can I help you with anything, Tony?"

He didn't answer, couldn't answer. His answer would be too large, too much for her. She was never going to be ready to marry him. Vita's look across the silence told him she was not ever going to return to where they'd been, that place he'd never left where she would never return. "I'm sorry," he stammered and rushed out. He noticed nothing on his return to the Morris. If there was any color to the sky, birds, or winter berries, hawks alight or tiny beasts below, all were a blur to Tony. The wind pushed in from the north, his ears numbed, he tripped on jutting rocks seeing nothing.

Was it February? He couldn't say. His temper grew short. He argued with Jocco, avoided kids at the Morris, thrashed in his sleep. The arithmetic of his life tortured his soul. He stopped bothering to go to church.

It wasn't that Tony snapped. He unraveled. People who saw it happening didn't believe it. Or, like his poor mother, refused to believe it. When he grabbed the gun off the hook that morning of February 10th, Marie Babić assumed he was going out to get her a rabbit or two. She was punching down her bread dough as Tony came through the house, buttoned his coat, took Jocco's gun, slammed out the door.

He didn't say where he was going and he didn't say goodbye.

Two hours later the police came to her door to say Tony had shot himself and died instantly. First, he'd shot Vita, standing behind the counter at the grocery with a younger sister at her side. The younger sister was not hurt. Two kids in the store to buy candy also were not hurt, but Vita was in the hospital, the police said.

Marie Babić continued to make dinner for her boarders. She propped the baby on Tony's chair and said nothing to anyone, not even Jocco home from work, who chose to sit outside in the cold and drink a neighbor's moonshine straight from the bottle.

The evening paper reported the news: *Local Youth Kills Self, Shoots Girl.* Each letter in this headline measured one full inch, out-claiming liquor raids in Chicago, farmers opposing tariffs, and the continued search for a missing airman.

It all happened so fast. The chimes over the door, words exchanged, Vita asking Tony to leave, the gun then and shots. Vita had been hit in the abdomen, she was rushed to the hospital and had surgery to remove the bullet. She seemed to recover some that afternoon, to rally as the stock market had done so many times those past months. Her family sat in chairs in her hospital room, watched as she breathed normally and seemed to sleep. Then near eight p.m. her systems broke down, her blood pressure dropped suddenly, her heartbeat slowed. She turned her head ever so slightly toward her parents and siblings gathered around her. She did not speak but appeared to smile as though all were well. She'd always been the prettiest of the family and that remained true. It always remained true.

TRUTH

There's a lot that happens. When you put it all together, there's lots that happens. My brother Pete's been dead almost thirty years now and even baby Helen. One by one I said my lousy prayers to everyone in my family, sent them off to wherever they are. Every one of those send-offs was tough, from my dad on down, but the worst for me was Petey. His heart just quit on him, poor Pete, making jokes with me to the end. I planted some trees to remember him. Take care of them now, watch them grow.

I'm doing pretty good though. Still drive, still mow the grass, paint the fence, putter around. My lady friend, God hope she's the last, cooks for me once a week. Makes me park my shoes by the door and wear little slippers she bought. If Pete could see that, he'd take out his broom and play me a sad song, I'll tell you that. No polkas for those slippers by the door.

I don't remember the day Tony died. Not any of it and I never wanted to know, never asked what Ma did or Pa or the funeral, none of that. It's like I slept through it all even though I know I didn't. I was there. We were all there.

I had a best friend after the war—and for half my life—a guy named Alec, who was as much fun for me as Petey. Only Alec was smooth, easy walk, aftershave, collar open. Alec and I were two of a kind. We loved people, we loved a good time, and we went light on the surface of things, making girls laugh, teasing each other every minute. Later Alec ran into some problems with work and his wife cheating and somewhere in all that he had an accident. Car coming at him on the wrong side of a county road out in California where he lived then and Alec swerved to avoid the crash just when the other driver swerved in that same direction and they hit head-on. Terrible thing. The other guy died in a minute. But Alec lived. Something about angles and speed, lots about luck if you ask me. But the thing is, Alec remembered nothing about the actual crash or the hours after, how he got out of the car, the sound of metal crumpling, whether he screamed or kept smoking his cigarette. None of it. Nada. "Johnny," he'd say, "I couldn't even tell you if it was my fault." He knew it wasn't. They did an assessment, cops and experts and the like, but it was nothing Alec could tell you one way or the other. And that's how it is with me and Tony's dying.

My daughter asked me once, did the kids at school pick on me after what happened with Tony. I don't remember that either. I'm pretty sure they didn't but who's to say. Kids liked me, for one thing. And I just turned nine years old. What the hell do nine-year-olds know about the news, miners striking or drunks staggering or someone killing someone and himself? It just isn't on their minds. Kids at nine are thinking how much longer they have to wait to be done with the spelling list or how to pitch the ball faster, that kind of thing. So I said no when she asked. Better to think they didn't.

What I do remember is my mother. I've got a picture of her from before, sometime in 1928, when we were all there, all still home and alive, and she's almost smiling, the whole brood in nice clothes, girls with lace trim, me and my little brothers in sailor suits, my dad with his chin high like a king and Tony right next to him. Any picture you see of my mother after that, her eyes are sad as Jesus on the cross and that's a fact. Not saying she didn't have good days, didn't bake her bread, mutter her million prayers in whatever language came out of her mouth. But Ma looked sad every day of her life after Tony died.

My sister Anna told me Ma would cry for no reason. The fire would burn too low. A couple chickens in the yard would scrap. Once my baby sister pulled a hat off the hook and Ma started to cry. I asked Anna, so was it Tony's hat? She didn't know. And within a year Anna got married anyway and Katie right after. By then Petey and I were old enough to know our numbers were dwindling. We had no older brother and the two sisters we liked to tease were gone then too.

But the Morris Location was another kind of family. The older we got the more we lived our days out on the street with kids we'd known forever. Even now the kids from the Morris talk, we remember this one and that, faces that used to be so much to us. It's the thing, seeing people you always knew. It's not the wrinkled guy there griping about the high school hockey team or the price of eggs at Super One, that's not who you see, but the kid before, with shaggy Depression hair and half his teeth still breaking through, high-water pants and holes in his shoes. That's who you see. Pete's wife grew up out there right next to us and that's what we discuss to this day. I stop to have coffee, she gives me a donut, and we tell our tales of the Morris which has been gone already more than half my life. While I was away in the service, the mining company needed that ore right where the Morris was built. So they tore it down and dug and all the families that lived there had to find somewhere else. Even so, none of us really left it.

One thing my parents did I never understood, they put up a shrine for Tony. We had no money and then there was this four-foot burial stone, white and grand with a picture of Tony in a little frame next to the last name Babić. I'm going to tell you, I couldn't get over that. The older I got, the more I wanted to forget we ever had a brother Tony, a goddamn hero in his time who brought trouble on himself and broke Ma's heart and Mrs. Markovic's heart as well. Why put up his picture for all to see and keep him alive that way? What was it to go out to the cemetery and see that?

And I'll tell you after my parents died, it got worse for me, seeing that picture on the stone. I never said a word. Pete wasn't one to discuss the world, let me tell you. We never sat eye to eye and turned the whole thing over and over. Georgie same way. In later years, my brother Nikko had a hundred notions I didn't really want to hear about and after a while, I didn't talk about it with my sisters either. When I got married, my wife asked who is this brother Anthony Joseph who died in 1930, and I said that's it, he died and we don't talk about it. She never asked me again. If she learned more than that, if one of my sisters told her the whole story, my wife didn't let on to me.

But when I was the last, when I was the one to scrub the stone clean white again and put out the flowers, what I did was—I took off Tony's picture. I pried it off. The stone was black under the frame, so I cleaned that with everything I could think of. If you go out to that stone now, you can still see the shadow, but that's all you see. You don't have to look at a handsome young guy and wonder how the hell he died when there wasn't even a war. You don't have to think about it, that's what I'm saying. On the ground the markers are overgrown with grass. If you want to see the names of Joseph, Marie, and Anthony Babić, you have to dust away the weeds and soot first. And who's going to do that?

I don't feel bad that I pulled Tony's picture off. They're all gone now and I can think whatever I want to think. When I was a kid, I missed him. When I grew up, I felt ashamed. I can't say for sure that any of my brothers or sisters had that shame. The girls prayed so much they maybe raised him to heaven anyway and let it go at that. The boys, I don't know. Except for Pete, they brought their own shame on one way or another. So I don't know. But what I want to tell you is that I don't feel that way now. I'm too old to care about shame. Now if I care and sometimes I care, it's about why. I mean I sit here and think about why. Because Tony was a good guy. Not funny like

Pete or shrewd like Nikko, Tony was smart and nice, the kind of kid you say, what a nice guy. Kind of guy you want working next to you or on your ball team. I guess I said all that before. He was something special. Tony was not the guy to do what he did.

But he did.

Ma blamed it on Chicago. We knew this cop there used to live with us, used to be a miner and a boarder, nice-looking guy from Croatia and kind of Ma's favorite the girls told me. What did I remember? I wasn't even old enough to go to school then, but Tony took to him and a couple years later went to visit him in Chicago—which I do remember, Tony packing his bag and heading off on a train like a grown-up, leaving me and Pete wandering around for days without him, no big brother and Ma praying the whole time he was gone. This cop, Luka was his name, wrote letters to Tony after that and maybe Ma thought he had some influence. "Got shooters in Chicago," she said the summer Tony went to visit and I remember that, too, because when you're a kid the age I was then, shooters in Chicago sounds pretty interesting, sounds like what you want to do, too, grab a gun and shoot criminals in some dark, smoky place like what might be Chicago.

My sister Margaret said this Luka would not have

been a bad influence. Maybe Jesus told her that. Or some saint. Anyway she never blamed Tony's death on Luka. But over the years my older sisters talked about it, this cop, the guns, Tony young with ideas. You don't want to think a guy you loved like we all loved Tony goes out and makes trouble on his own. You want to think it's someone else. Something outside Tony. That appealed to my family, though my mother never said so directly. Pa neither. At least not that I heard.

Then this cop Luka had some fame after that. Maybe it was fame. Living in Timbuktu like we were, lots of things looked like fame. This Luka, he went to work for the FBI or whatever the feds had going on in the early thirties. He went from being a cop to being a fed and was part of the team brought down Dillinger. That's the story. Luka helped bring down the biggest criminal we knew back then, a bank robber who killed and raised hell wherever he went and was gunned down in the street. Mining people love a story like that, let me tell you. Who doesn't want to think they knew a Croatian cop helped bring down John Dillinger?

Anna told me Margaret wrote to Luka to tell him what happened to Tony, and Luka wrote back right away to say how sad he was, it must be the Depression got to him or love or something that wasn't the Tony he knew. Luka wrote to Margaret that the Tony he knew was one of the smartest, sweetest guys he ever met. Honest to God. That's what Anna told me. He wrote a note to my parents, too, Anna said, but whatever they did with it, the rest of us never saw. If any of the girls found that note from Luka, we'd all have heard about it, you can bet on that.

Luka saying it might have been the Depression, that's not the worst idea either. We never had much, but after the stock market crashed, life on the Iron Range got worse, let me tell you. When things aren't being built, when people don't buy cars and companies don't make ships or trucks or trains, then the mines slow down and that's what they did. I was eight years old at the time it started, so when I think about being a kid, it's mostly that, a time when there wasn't enough, when we drank too much tea for want of something better, wore out our shoes, made hockey sticks out of anything we could swing at a chunk of wood in the street. I think of soups and mended socks and mended pants and haircuts sitting in the kitchen. Ma's prayers. An apple each for Christmas. And most of the Depression, Tony was already gone.

But he'd lost his job, so that was what the Depression did to Tony. He lost his job and he lost his girl and then he wasn't even Tony anymore. The Morris kids played on without him. Me and Pete still followed him all over the place, but after he lost that job, maybe he didn't tease us back anymore. One thing fades to another, that's the thing. Tony was our hero and when he quit school, he was still our hero. Don't ask when he stopped being our hero. There's no actual point, no actual day when I knew that my brother Tony wasn't a hero. No day I remember anyway. It wasn't the day he died. It wasn't the day he was buried. It was the day, whenever that was, when I wished he weren't my brother. Pete and I, we were on our own then. After that I was always on my own. I had my brothers and friends all my life. I always have friends, I know how to make friends, but bottom line as they say, bottom line, I was on my own. I couldn't claim Tony and then I couldn't even claim how much a hero he was to me and so where was I then? On my own. Maybe that's just growing up. Pretty soon, there's nobody looking out for Johnny, where's Johnny, does he have a scarf around his neck in winter or socks on his feet or oatmeal in his belly? Pretty soon, you got to take care of all that on your own.

But I never lost a job in my life. I only got jobs. I got jobs and then I got better jobs and every job I had I did well and I knew it. I don't know how Tony would have felt losing his job at Oliver Mining just when he was starting out. Men need their jobs, I'll tell you that. More than once in my life those mines went on strike and I took off every time for work wherever I could find it. I spent one summer in Bemidji welding for a small company and another long stretch doing maintenance for my brother-in-law's industrial laundry in Fargo. Wherever I had to go, whatever I had to do, I had a family to support and I needed to work. Tony didn't have a family. But he had his pride. A guy like Tony always had pride. That's why it's so hard to believe, everything that happened.

And it came on like a storm, that Depression. Everything was just rolling along and then it wasn't. That's what the older guys would say. Like Pearl Harbor. We got caught having a good old time and then we were clobbered. Tony quit school to work and not even a year later he got let go. Then what? There were no extra jobs just waiting around for some kid to step in and save the day. And there was Vita over in the grocery store with her family and her high school education, not wanting to hang out with Tony anymore for whatever reason, love being something that can come and go like spring flowers. Maybe it was her old man. Maybe it was another guy. Maybe it was just a pretty girl looking forward to something else. I don't hold her to any of those reasons because I just don't know. Poor Vita. She had everything ahead of her—and then she didn't.

Margaret said Ma went over to the grocery afterward. I don't know when afterward, how long afterward, but they were friends, her and Mrs. Marković, and Vita's mom accepted that visit, took in Ma's apology mother to mother. That's what Margaret said. Vita's middle name was Therese and after Ma's visit to Mrs. Marković, Ma decided our baby sister would take that same middle name, which might not seem much, but back then a name was something you could offer that didn't cost you money and gave respect, honor even, and lived on. That was the whole point. Vita's middle name lived on in my baby sister. And I'm sure my sister knew the story. I'm sure she prayed all her life for Vita Therese Marković.

The building's still there in Brooklyn where now half the houses been torn down for want of care. But there it is, brown stucco with those wide store windows and crabgrass growing all around. Old Man Marković probably rolling over in his grave to see that place he put all his life into until the big groceries took over. That happened I'm thinking mid-sixties when the store next door to us closed up and the old lady took off for Florida. Half a block down they closed years before, about the time my wife and I were married and settling in, and the Italians that owned the place said they'd sell us their store for seven thousand dollars. Seven grand with an apartment to live upstairs, a garage apartment to rent out in the back, and practically next door to my in-laws. I remember that. Seven grand. But my wife and I moved into my in-law's duplex and paid them rent for thirty years. Which was fine with me. I was never big on mortgages and banks.

It's a wreck now, that old Marković store. Thing about stucco, it lasts forever, but everything else falls apart around it—windows rot, the roof decays, doors hang half-assed, steps sag. Used to be I wouldn't go anywhere near that store or if I did drive past it, I'd look out the window in the other direction, fiddle with the radio dial, anything not to look at that place. Now I go by once a week maybe. Maybe more. I drive home from bocce that way sometimes or when I'm coming home from the opposite end of the Iron Range. Now it's like a magnet pulling me over there to look at that place with its empty windows and crummy brown stucco. It's like I'm going to know something just driving by the place where my brother Tony showed up in the middle of a winter day with that goddamned gun in his hand.

The gun's the thing. All the other theories—cops in Chicago and the Depression, losing his job and losing his girl, love gone wrong, you name it—they all come back to the gun. Pa hung a gun on the wall to keep those boarders away from the girls. So there it was. You wonder my smart old man never thought that maybe one of the boarders could just as easily grab that gun and shoot anyone in the house, girl or no girl. You wonder Pa just hung it there year after year not thinking no good would come of it. But he was in charge. The gun was his. So he thought nobody else would touch it, and until Tony, maybe nobody ever did.

I've got guns. Got them right now as I speak, zipped into heavy-duty cases that are locked and those cases up on the top shelf above the stove in a cupboard that's locked and that's the way I've always done it and that's the way I always will. I've got hunting rifles, that's what I've got. After the Depression and the war, most guys knew the need to hunt food for their families, stock away meat and fish for the long seasons. Ladies canned their vegetables and fruits and guys brought home partridges and deer. That's how we knew to get by back then. Every penny counted. Seven grand bought you a store with a garage apartment. That's what I'm saying.

But my kids never saw a gun hanging on a hook in the house, I'll tell you that right now. The place for guns is where you have to drag a stepladder out to reach them.

When they got Dillinger, he drew out a Colt 1908 to

defend himself. Lot of good it did him. Lot of good that gun did Tony or my family. I'm no fool. I see what I see. These guys out there shooting people left and right like they got a war going on and anyone's fair game. You can say the same thing about them as about my brother. Maybe they lost a job or couldn't get one. Maybe they're depressed like Nikko used to say Tony was depressed. Maybe they lost their girl or somebody pissed them off or the sun didn't come up quick enough that day or they drank too much or they read about gangs in Chicago or New York or California where they're all half nuts anyway. Maybe this, maybe that. In the end, you look in the mirror and there you are. Just you. It's you that does whatever you do and makes your life whatever it is and craps it out if that's what happens. Like I said, there's lots that happens.

Then if there's a gun right there for you, just hanging on the wall right there for you, in that one lousy minute maybe that's what you do. You go for the gun. And that's the end of the story.

STEEL

ACKNOWLEDGEMENTS

The historical references in *Steel*, including newspaper head-lines, events and places, were researched through the Hibbing Historical Society, the Iron Range Research Center, the Minnesota Historical Society, and the *Chicago Tribune* archives.

KATHLEEN NOVAK

is a poet and writer who grew up on the iron mining range of Northern Minnesota, the granddaughter of Italian and Croatian immigrants. She is the author of the Minnesota Book Award finalist *Do Not Find Me* and its companion, *The Autobiography of Corrine Bernard: A Novel*, which was selected as a semifinalist for the Chautauqua Prize in 2019. Her novel of small-town characters in mid-century America, *Rare Birds*, was released in 2017. Ms. Novak's poems have been published in literary magazines nationally. She lives in Minneapolis.

www.kathleennovak.com

CPSIA information can be obtained
at www.ICGtesting.com
Printed in the USA
BVHW040959240222
630007BV00015B/897

9 781734 229899